"This Isn't Funny. This City Will Support A Specialty Store Like Mine—Barely. But Not If There's Two Of Us."

Mac grinned. "So the way you see it, ma'am, this town's not big enough for the both of us."

"But we have a problem here," Hilary said clearly. "And don't just shrug."

He shrugged. "You don't think I'm cute when I shrug?"

Hilary sniffed.

"I'm sorry. I can see this is important to you. We have things to talk about—how about dinner tonight?" Mac proposed.

Hilary's voice was cool. "Do you have someplace in mind?"

He answered without missing a beat. "Domingo's, up on Bank Street."

She recognized the name. A Caribbean place. "I take it your interest in hot sauce is more than just professional."

"You bet. And yours?"

"I never met a chili pepper I couldn't handle," Hilary responded.

Dear Reader,

Happy 1992, and welcome to Silhouette Desire! For those of you who are new readers, I must say I think you're starting the year off right—with wonderful romance. If you're a regular Desire fan, you already know what delicious stories are in store for you . . . this month *and* this year. I wish I could tell you the exciting things planned for you in 1992, but that would be giving all of my secrets away. But I will admit that it's going to be a great year.

As for January, what better way to kick off a new year of *Man of the Month* stories than with a sensuous, satisfying love story from Ann Major, *A Knight in Tarnished Armor*. And don't miss any of 1992's *Man of the Month* books, including stories written by Diana Palmer, Annette Broadrick, Dixie Browning, Sherryl Woods and Laura Leone—and that's just half of my lineup!

This month is completed with books by Barbara Boswell, Beverly Barton, Cathryn Clare, Jean Barrett and Toni Collins. They're all terrific; don't miss a single one.

And remember, don't hesitate to write and tell me what you think of the books. I'm always glad to receive reader feedback.

So go wild with Desire . . . until next month,

Lucia Macro
Senior Editor

CATHRYN CLARE

HOT STUFF

SILHOUETTE *Desire*®

Published by Silhouette Books New York

America's Publisher of Contemporary Romance

SILHOUETTE BOOKS
300 East 42nd St., New York, N.Y. 10017

HOT STUFF

ISBN: 0-373-05688-5

First Silhouette Books printing January 1992

Printed in the U.S.A.

Books by Cathryn Clare

Silhouette Desire

To the Highest Bidder #399
Blind Justice #508
Lock, Stock and Barrel #550
Five by Ten #591
The Midas Touch #663
Hot Stuff #688

CATHRYN CLARE

is a transplanted Canadian who moved south of the border after marrying a far-from-proper Bostonian. She and her husband now live in an old house in central Massachusetts, where she divides her time between writing and renovating. "Three cats and a view of the forest outside my office window help with the writing part," she says.

With thanks to Lisa Lammé at Le Saucier in Boston,
and to Fred, whose asbestos palate never ceases to amaze.

One

The same thing had been happening all day, and it was beginning to get on Hilary Gardiner's nerves.

She'd figured her small shop would be busy on opening day, filled with friends and acquaintances who had come to check the place out and wish her well on her new venture. And her well-placed advertising had, as she'd hoped, drawn in a good number of strangers, some neighbors and a few tourists who'd tracked down her out-of-the-way location. She was enjoying chatting with them, while listening to the gratifying sound of the cash register ringing in the background.

What she hadn't figured on was the way all her random conversations seemed to keep turning in the direction of Ste. Helene.

"This is a lovely little place," a woman was telling her now, glancing around the rows of brightly colored jars and bottles. "But I didn't see any food from Ste. Helene. Don't you carry it?"

For what felt like the tenth time, Hilary launched into her explanation of how it had been impossible to import things from Ste. Helene ever since the military coup on the small Caribbean island. "At one time Ste. Helene and Canada were very friendly," she said, "but now it seems the military doesn't want anything to do with us. It's too bad, with all these Ste. Helenean restaurants springing up all over and everybody interested in their food all of a sudden, but I just haven't been able to import any of it."

"Where do the restaurants get their supplies?" the woman wanted to know.

Hilary had wondered the same thing, but so far she hadn't had time to track down the answer. "I'm not sure," she admitted. "I imagine the Ste. Helenean refugees who run them have some kind of connections back home." She made a mental note to follow up on the question first thing next week. If Ste. Helenean food was this popular, she'd better figure out a way to get on the bandwagon fast, for the sake of her fledgling business.

That was when the woman dropped her bombshell. "Oh, well," she said casually, "maybe they just buy things from that guy down in the Byward Market."

Hilary felt her neck stiffen. "What guy?" she asked. She'd done the most thorough market research possible in the course of the past year, and she thought she knew every specialty food store in Ottawa.

"He just opened today, same as you," the woman said. "In fact, we just came from there. We're doing kind of a grand food tour."

Hilary carefully set down the plate of samples she was holding. "So this place sells Caribbean food, does it?" she asked. She lifted a hand as if to brush a stray hair away from her face—a needless gesture, since her shiny black hair was pulled neatly back in its customary ponytail. It was a nervous habit, she realized, and wished she didn't feel so uneasy.

"Oh, no," the woman said brightly. "Just hot sauce, like you."

Hilary's sense of unease was ballooning inside her. "And he just opened today," she echoed. Ottawa wasn't that big a city, in spite of being the nation's capital. One little specialty shop selling hot sauce had a chance of making a go of it, but the idea of competition was making some size extra-large butterflies start to cavort around in her stomach.

Especially if the competition was selling trendy products that she couldn't get. She frowned again, noticing the woman was getting ready to leave. "What was his shop like?" she asked the patron, trying not to sound too anxious.

"Not nearly as nicely done up as this," the woman said. "I love the way you've got things displayed in the window, so the light shines through them. The place in the market is a lot darker, and—I guess 'rustic' would be a nice way to put it."

Well, that was something, Hilary thought. But it wasn't everything. "Was he busy?" she forced herself to ask.

"Packed," the woman said. "It seems like all the tourists head for the market, doesn't it? I guess it's in a pretty good location."

Good enough that it had been far out of Hilary's price range when she'd rented space for her store, she thought glumly as she watched the woman pay for a couple of small jars of barbecue sauce. Suddenly the high hopes she'd had when she'd opened the doors this morning seemed very shaky indeed.

She didn't like the feeling. She'd spent too much of her life scrambling to keep things together, hustling to get to a point where she was the one in control. She'd be darned if she was going to let some stranger get the jump on her like this.

She forced a smile back onto her face as a new round of people entered the store. She picked up her tray of samples and headed to greet them, but in the back of her mind she was worrying over the problem the tourist had so casually dropped on her. By four-thirty, her feet were aching, her shelves were pleasingly depleted, and the store was finally quiet enough for her to be able to think through what she needed to do.

"Mom, look!"

Her son Todd was ringing open the cash register for her to see, pointing to its contents as though he'd struck gold. Hilary had to smile when she looked at him. He and his twin brother were tall for fourteen, already taller than her own five foot six. They'd inherited her black hair and fair skin, and she knew for a fact that their dark good looks made them the heartthrobs of half the girls at school.

"We made enough today so we can all retire," Todd was proclaiming, showing her the cash drawer.

"It's a nice thought, kiddo," she told him, "but I wouldn't start booking expensive vacations quite yet, if I were you. Don't forget, not every day is going to be like this."

"Aw, Mom, you're too cautious. Isn't she, Andrew?"

Todd's mirror image, Andrew, appeared from the back room. Hilary wished she could remember what it felt like to be fourteen years old and unaware of such adult oddities as mortgage payments and bank loan applications.

"She can be cautious if she wants to. People really liked the store, though." Methodical Andrew had appointed himself in charge of inventory control, a job he took very seriously. "I heard a lot of good comments, Mom. And we're going to need to restock a lot of this stuff pretty soon."

"Good. Maybe if we move some of the stock out, we'll be able to sit down on the furniture again." Hilary smiled tiredly, picturing the stacks of crates and boxes that had taken over their living room in the past few weeks. Lacking a stockroom, she'd been forced to turn her small home into a warehouse.

She looked at her sons again. They were so enthusiastic about this store, and so certain it would be, in Todd's phrase, a megahit. She'd sunk every penny into *Fortissimo*. Andrew had chosen the name. The venture had her sons' full approval, but sometimes the size of the risk she was taking made her wonder if she was crazy.

The thought of her unknown competitor downtown didn't help at all. *Fortissimo* had the potential to be a megaflop if what the informative tourist had told her was correct.

Hilary turned to the third member of her volunteer staff. "Karen," she said, "I have to run downtown for a little while. Do you think you can handle closing up for me?"

"Sure thing, boss." Karen looked up from the mailing list that people had been signing all day. "I'll get the boys to walk to the bank with me when I make the deposit."

"You're an angel." Hilary grabbed her purse from the small back room, already fishing in it for her car keys. "I won't be long, and when I come back we can have our celebration dinner."

The boys cheered in chorus, and Karen, a classmate from Hilary's business course at the University of Ottawa and now a close friend, grinned at her. "You just said the magic word," she said. "Don't rush, Hilary. I'll close up at five and we'll meet you at home."

The trip to Ottawa's Byward Market took twice as long as it should have. Hilary knew, of course, that tomorrow was Canada Day, and that the capital city would be packed. It was the reason she'd pushed so hard to get her store open by this weekend. She'd enjoyed thinking of the hordes of tourists as potential customers, but maneuvering around them on the crowded streets was a lot less fun.

The Byward Market sat in the middle of the old part of Ottawa, its buildings flanked by open-air stalls selling produce and flowers. Usually Hilary let herself get caught up in the market's appeal when she came down here shopping for vegetables. Today she found herself cursing the crowds and muttering unkind things when she discovered that one parking garage after another was crammed full of cars already.

She finally found a barely legal parking space not far from the central market building, and began a hurried tour of the area. She felt a little like a spawning salmon, trying desperately to swim upstream. All the tourists seemed to want to go in the opposite direction, and the crush of bodies made it difficult to look around. By the time she'd satisfied herself that her competitor wasn't in the main building, she was hot and tired and wondering if she shouldn't leave her crazy quest until next week.

Then she remembered how heavily invested she was in her own shop, and how everything—including the money for her sons' university educations—depended on her making a go of *Fortissimo.* She straightened her shoulders and plunged into the crowds circling the central building.

She found the place almost by accident. There was no sign outside, and a scant attempt at a display in the front window. The stack of crates behind the plate glass looked more like the chaos in her living room than the elegant window display at *Fortissimo.* She'd barely registered the fact that one of the crates had Ste. Helene stamped on the side of it when her eyes shifted to the flamboyant red dress of the woman coming out of the store.

The woman was tall, with skin the color of coffee beans. Her dazzling white teeth flashed as she spoke in rapid French to someone in the store. Hilary slowed as all those facts registered. Ste. Helene had been in the news a lot when the military coup had occurred, and that particular brilliant shade of red had been a favorite with the thousands of people who'd come to Canada as refugees.

Hilary took a deep breath, and waited until the woman moved away. Then she smoothed her hands on her skirt—her summer-weight ivory dress seemed very pale suddenly, compared to that blazing Ste. Helenean red—and entered the store.

It was like walking into the cabin of an old-fashioned sailing ship. She wasn't sure what gave her that impression. Maybe it was the dark wood of the walls, or the unorganized stacks of wooden crates piled throughout the place, partially blocking the light from outside.

Or maybe it was the fact that there was a pirate standing there looking at her.

Hilary blinked. She wasn't given to fanciful imaginings—her mind just didn't work that way. And certainly there was nothing in the man's clothes to suggest piracy. He was wearing ordinary blue jeans, obviously well-worn and a little threadbare around the knees and the crease of his hips. His T-shirt was a plain white one, a little tight across his shoulders. Hardly standard pirate attire.

And yet the instant she saw him she felt as though she were standing in a sea breeze, salty, sharp and free. She could practically see the renegade black flag.

It was ridiculous. She was a thousand miles from the ocean, in familiar, slightly understated Ottawa. How was it that the sparkle in a pair of hazel eyes could do this to her? There was something in the slant of his eyebrow, and his casual stance, strong thighs braced as though the deck of an ocean-going ship were rolling beneath his feet, that made her taste salt and freedom on her own tongue.

"Can I help you?"

It wasn't what she'd expected the pirate to say, and the ordinary phrase brought her back to dry land in a hurry. If this was the owner of the chaotic little shop, he'd pirated her idea, and threatened her livelihood. No doubt that was why he struck her as more buccaneer than businessman.

"I thought I'd just come in and have a look around," she said, wanting to check things out without letting him know who she was. "You haven't been open very long, have you?"

"Just opened this morning," he said cheerfully. "As a matter of fact, as you can probably tell, I'm still unpacking boxes." He stepped past her to the doorway and flipped over the Open sign so that it said Closed. "I figured I'd call it a day at five-thirty," he explained. "But don't feel you have to rush. I've had a crowd in here all day, and I'm looking forward to getting some work done in peace and quiet."

Hilary frowned. She and Karen had been up well past midnight making sure *Fortissimo* was in order for today's grand opening. Her competition hadn't even bothered to clear a path from the door to the cash register, or to plan in advance what his opening hours were going to be. She sidestepped a pile of boxes and began to wander through the store.

The man pulled a utility knife from his back pocket, and for half a second Hilary expected him to grasp it between his teeth and go swarming up the rigging. Instead, he started cutting open cardboard boxes, as he'd obviously been doing before she walked in.

Why did she keep thinking of him as a pirate? Was it the way his short, slightly curly brown hair seemed to have been stirred by an unseen breeze just a moment before? Or was it that athletic build—not stocky, but very fit—and the golden tan that spoke of many years under the tropical sun, far removed from Ottawa winters?

She forced herself to keep moving, to stop staring at him. She was entitled to feel curious about the man, she knew. He was, after all, in a position to undercut everything she'd worked so hard for. But she knew what she was doing came perilously close to ogling, and that was unlike Hilary Gardiner.

"Looking for anything in particular?" She could see the strength of his forearms as he slashed open a crate with his knife. "Believe it or not, I *do* know where everything is, in spite of the mess."

"I was interested in some things from Ste. Helene," Hilary replied guardedly. "Do you have any of that *poivre* sauce?"

"Actually on the island we say *poive*. Got a whole carton of it here somewhere." His sudden grin caught her off guard. She was looking sideways at him when he smiled, and the whiteness of his teeth against his tanned skin was like the sparkle of sun on blue water.

She felt a perverse urge to see if he really *did* know where all his stock was. "I'd appreciate it if you could dig some out," she said. "I've been looking everywhere for it."

"It's pretty hard to get. Even I had a hard time with this order." He folded his knife and stuck it back in his jeans pocket. Hilary couldn't help following the motion, and her eyes lingered on the slim hips encased in old denim even after their owner had crossed the room with his easy, long-legged gait.

It took a minute for his words to register. "What do you mean, 'even you' had a hard time?" she asked him. "Do you have a special dispensation or something?"

There was a twinge of tension in her voice, and he seemed to hear it. He shot her another glance, minus the engaging grin this time, and explained, "I used to work on Ste. Helene, before the coup. I still have some connections there. That's how I can get things out of the country, although I admit it took some finagling."

He must have been a sailor, she thought. That would account for the easy stride, the tanned skin, the general air that the world could think what it liked about him and he didn't give a damn.

"What were you doing down there?" she asked. She was surprised at her own boldness.

He lifted an eyebrow, then started hefting the top cartons in the pile and started a new pile on the floor. "This and that," he said briefly.

"I see." What she saw was that he had no intention of giving her the details. With that devil-may-care gleam in his eye and the X-rated way his jeans hugged his hips when he walked, he might have been anything from a venture capitalist to a soldier of fortune.

She gave her head a little shake. It was business, not body language, that she'd come to check out.

The muscles in her back gave a sympathetic twinge every time he lifted a carton, as she thought of all the boxes she'd lifted herself in the past week. She knew how heavy they were, and yet her mysterious pirate barely seemed to feel the weight of them. Finally he came to what he was looking for, another wooden crate labeled Ste. Helene.

"Here we go," he said, lifting the crate and carrying it over to the counter. Hilary followed him, her eyes drawn irresistibly to the way his arm muscles tensed and his strong fingers grasped the edges of the rough wooden crate. She was so mesmerized by that golden tanned skin that it took a moment to register that instead of the gentle clinking of bottles in the carton, there was the sound of broken glass rattling around.

He realized it at the same moment. With a muttered expletive, he reached for a small crowbar on the counter and quickly pried the top off the crate. They bent their heads together to look inside, and for a moment and a half Hilary had a flashback to the unsettling feeling she'd had when she first came in. Something about the simple act of brushing her own sleek black head against his tousled one made the floor rock gently, like a ship at anchor tugging to get free.

Her companion's muttering got a little more explicit when he saw what shape his cargo was in. "Well, hell," he said, reaching inside and pulling out a cracked glass bottle. "And I've only got two cartons of this stuff, too. I can't believe it."

He pulled out a couple of intact bottles, but the rest were either cracked or broken. The bottom of the crate was swimming in the pungent sauce that was the island's trademark. The peppery aroma made Hilary's senses sit up and take notice.

"That's what I get for hiring fly-by-night shippers, I guess," he said ruefully. "It'll take me six weeks to get another order in."

Hilary watched him closely. His reaction was peculiar. His annoyance was already fading, as if the smashed shipment meant nothing to him. In his position, she'd be frantically checking the rest of the boxes, calculating how much she'd lost, and worrying over what the damage to a popular item would do to her business. This man seemed willing to let it all go by with a shrug.

"You know," she said slowly, "the common wisdom in the business world is to check for damage before you pay off your shipper. That way it's his responsibility, not yours."

"Guess that'll teach me, won't it?" He'd dipped one finger into the spilled sauce, and was licking it off as he spoke. Hilary knew how piquant the island spices were, and she felt her lips tingling as she watched him.

"That's a pretty funny reaction," she said. "I mean, what if I'd come here specifically to spend a lot of money on *poive* sauce, and now you discover you don't have any to sell me? Doesn't that worry you?"

For the first time he looked closely at her, and she was startled by the sudden scrutiny. "That's a pretty funny question," he said, considering her.

"I don't think it is," she replied. "Aren't you mad about those broken bottles?"

"Why cry over spilled hot sauce?" He grinned and lifted his shoulders, but she saw the perceptive gleam in his eyes intensify. She had an uneasy feeling he was now finding her as interesting as she found him.

"Not even when it means you lose money, and maybe customers?"

This time his scrutiny was silent. He seemed to be taking in the inquisitorial tone of her voice. After a moment he picked up the two bottles that had survived the wreckage, wiped them off with a paper towel, and handed them to her.

"Here," he said. "If you're so worried about it, you can have these gratis. They're a little gooey, but they're all yours with my compliments."

"That's not what I meant." She was beginning to be inexplicably annoyed with the man, contrasting his cavalier way of doing business with her own careful calculations. "I just wonder how long you're going to stay in business, if you're this nonchalant about a damaged shipment that you can't easily replace."

He shrugged again. The movement loosened his T-shirt at the waistband of his jeans, and Hilary felt her eyes being tugged in that direction. She wondered where he'd gotten the old brass buckle he wore on his belt. She wondered if his hands were as strong and warn as they looked.

She wondered if breathing the escaped fumes of the broken hot sauce bottles was affecting her mind. She'd barely looked sideways at a man since her husband had left her, almost eleven years ago. And now she couldn't keep her eyes off this stranger, even while she was getting more and more irritated with him.

"You know, for a casual shopper you seem pretty concerned about my business," he was saying. His voice had a slight rasp to it, in spite of its mellowness. "Did you really just come in here to spend a lot of money on *poive* sauce?"

"I came in to see your store," she hedged, realizing she wasn't going to be able to put him off with polite excuses. "Someone told me you'd just opened, and I was interested."

The gleam in his hazel eyes was stronger now. She had a feeling he was seeing right through her. The thought made her stand up a little straighter.

His next question was a surprise. "What's your name, anyway?" he asked.

"Hilary," she said. "Hilary Gardiner."

"It's too old for you."

She was startled. "What are you talking about?" she asked.

He leaned one elbow on the glass-topped counter and looked at her. "When you walked in here, at first I thought you were some teenager playing dress-up," he said. "And then I thought you were an unusually poised twenty-year-old. And now that I look at you up close, I think you must be nearer to thirty. But you still look like a damn teenager. Hilary's too grown-up sounding for you."

The deck was tilting under her feet again with a vengeance now. Somehow, with half a dozen sentences and a devilishly perceptive hazel-eyed stare, he'd managed to turn this whole visit into something personal.

"I'm thirty-two," she blurted, using the words like a barrier against his charm.

"You can't be."

She didn't tell him she had the fourteen-year-old sons to prove it. Pulling herself up a little straighter, she assured him, "On days like this I feel every day of it, believe me."

"All right, I believe you. You're a thirty-two-year-old teenager, and if you stand up any straighter your spine's going to start creaking."

He was laughing at her now. He seemed to have forgotten the broken bottles and his suspicions of her. Somehow she'd almost forgotten them herself. Deciding to turn the tables on him, she demanded, "And what's your name?"

"John Augustus Laurier MacDougall."

He recited the names with a flourish, and she was still wondering why they sounded vaguely familiar when he added, with a grin, "But my friends call me Mac."

"Did your friends tell you that the common wisdom is to get your storefront into shape *before* you open your doors?"

His grin only widened. "My friends know me too well to bother complaining about my housekeeping style," he told her. "Although one particularly brave soul did suggest that by the time I got all the boxes unpacked, my year would be up and it would be time to close the place again."

"Your year? Did someone grant you a magic wish or something, and does the store turn into a pumpkin by next July 1?" It wouldn't have surprised her, somehow.

Mac threw back his head and laughed. No, he wasn't the stuff of fairy tales, she decided. His laugh was far too earthy, and too real.

"I guess I should have spent a little longer on my window display," he said. "It's all spelled out there, but nobody seems to be noticing it."

He led the way to the front of the dark little store, and yanked at something that was draped across the boxes in the crowded front window. When he'd hauled it inside, Hilary could see that it was a four-foot-long banner, in vibrant Ste. Helenean red. It was boldly hand lettered, and it read: "MAC'S HOT STUFF. 'Open one year only. Get it while you can.'"

Hilary felt her own eyebrows raise. "You've got to be kidding," she said.

"What? Not big enough? I figured if it was red, it would catch the eye. Maybe if I polished the glass—"

"Polishing the glass wouldn't be a bad idea, but that wasn't what I was talking about. What on earth kind of businessman opens a store just for one year? Everybody in the retail trade knows you need longevity to make a go of things."

He shrugged. "I figured maybe I could substitute trendiness for longevity," he said. "I'm not very good at staying in one place for very long. I'd get bored doing the same thing for more than a year."

Hilary clenched her teeth to keep from saying *How about running my business into the ground? Would that be boring for you?* "Well, you seem to have picked the right trend," she said tightly.

"That's the truth. I knew stuff from Ste. Helene was popular, but not this popular. Store's been full all day. Anyway, I thought if I had a product people wanted, and an imposed deadline for the availability of the product, it would make the place a guaranteed hit."

That went contrary to all the good principles of business Hilary had just spent several years learning. She'd also learned, however, that there were certain people with enough nerve and enough luck to get away with bending the rules. Unfortunately for her, John Augustus Laurier MacDougall looked like he might be one of those people.

"I take it you don't need to do this to make money."

She couldn't help saying it. Her own small savings were invested so deeply in *Fortissimo*. She *had* to worry about every broken bottle, whether she wanted to or not. And she had to survive for more than a year, which might be impossible if this handsome buccaneer stuck around.

"What does it matter why I'm doing it?" He crossed his arms over his chest, suddenly looking defensive. Hilary decided she liked him better when he was joking, but a part of her was glad they'd gotten to business at last.

"Mr. MacDougall," she began, and then realized it sounded all wrong. The man wasn't a Mr. MacDougall and probably never would be. "Mac," she amended, and then went on, "I'm going to be perfectly straight with you. You're not the only one starting a new business today. I just opened one of my own, over on Wellington Street."

He nodded, waiting. Hilary swallowed past an unexpected obstacle in her throat.

"You'll never guess what I sell," she said, and heard her voice quaver ever so slightly.

The quaver seemed to tip him off. "Not hot sauce," he said.

"I'm afraid so."

She expected him to be angry, as she'd been, or worried, as she still was. At the very least, she expected the kind of reaction he'd shown when he'd first found the broken bottles of *poive* sauce—brief, perhaps, but chagrined just the same.

What she got instead was a great guffaw, and it rendered her speechless. His laugh was as full of life as his taut, athletic body, or the glint in his eyes, and for an instant she was caught up in listening to it. For an instant, she could see the joke through his eyes.

But only for an instant. "Damn it," she said. "This isn't funny. I don't know about you, but I've spent a lot of hours trying to figure out whether the demographics of the city will support a specialty item like hot sauce, and I decided that by a very slim margin, I can survive. But not if there's two of us."

He refused to stop grinning. He deepened his voice slightly, imitating a John Wayne drawl. "So the way you see it, ma'am, this town's not big enough for the both of us."

He was obviously enjoying the whole thing immensely. Hilary felt that lump in her throat again, and this time she couldn't swallow past it. It was bad enough to find that she had competition, but to find he wouldn't even take her seriously—

"How much market research did you do?" she asked pointedly.

He waved a hand casually. "Market research is boring," he proclaimed.

"You mean you didn't do *any?*" Hilary's voice rose a little as her disbelief crept into it. "You just plunk yourself down in a high-rent district like this without any preliminary work?"

Another casual shrug. "I like the Byward Market. I used to come here every Saturday when I was a kid. Why did you pick Wellington Street, anyway? It's a bit out of the way."

Hilary gritted her teeth. "I picked it because it's what I could afford," she said. "Of course I'd be here, too, if I had the money. Look, Mr. MacDougall—"

"A minute ago your were calling me Mac."

She knew it, but she'd changed her mind. She refused to be on a first-name basis with a man who could laugh at her dilemma like this. "Mr. MacDougall," she repeated clearly, "we have a problem here. And don't just shrug at me again, because I'm beginning to get very annoyed when you do that."

Of course, he shrugged. The cocky smile never left his face. "You don't think I'm cute when I shrug?" he asked.

The really annoying thing was that he *was* cute when he shrugged. No, not cute, she amended. He was sexier than any man she'd ever met, when the muscles of his shoulder pulled tight for an instant against the bright white of his T-shirt.

"I've been in contact with every business organization there is in Ottawa," Hilary went on, sticking to her train of thought with an effort. "If you'd talked to anybody—anybody at all—they could have told you you had competition. I can't believe you just opened up without even checking around."

He started to shrug, caught her eye and stopped. The laughter in the hazel depths of his eyes told her he was baiting her now. "I don't do business that way," he said.

She believed him. One look at John Augustus Laurier MacDougall told you this was a rogue who'd gotten by all his life on a combination of blarney, good luck and an innate sense of where the wind was blowing.

She, on the other hand, had learned by hard experience to check every step before she put her foot down. And even then it had taken a lot of work and a lot of heartache to get to the point where she was feeling halfway independent again.

And now this smiling vagabond had sailed into her life and threatened—in the nicest possible way—to take it all away from her. It wasn't fair, she thought, and felt the emotions churning inside start to reach their way to the surface. She didn't cry often, and never in front of strangers. But something in that smile of his made him seem so impervious. And just at the moment she felt far, far too vulnerable. She gave a cough that was intended to sound like a simple clearing of the throat, but which was really dangerously close to tears.

Mac was astonished by the sound. He'd guessed she had some hidden agenda the moment she'd walked in the door. He was adept at reading people, and there had been a sense of purpose in her elegant walk and up-tilted chin that didn't go with a routine shopping trip. He'd taken an unholy pleasure in drawing out her anger, because he had a sense in his bones that Hilary Gardiner was a woman who needed to loosen up, to laugh at herself, to see the humor in this absurd situation.

But now he realized he'd pushed things too far. She was genuinely upset.

"I'm sorry," he said, leaning toward her so that their faces were closer together. He was still amazed that a woman of thirty-two could come off looking not much past childhood. It went beyond that, he thought. There was something in her blue eyes that made him think she'd been cheated out of girlhood somehow, catapulted into the adult world before she was really ready. *That* was what had led him to try to make her laugh, as much as anything else.

"I'm sorry," he repeated. "I can see this is important to you."

She gave a sniff that almost but not quite covered up her feelings. "'Important' is one way to put it," she said. Her attempt at a smile was shaky.

Mac gave her the full benefit of his own smile. "I didn't realize," he said. "I guess I didn't think it through. My friends tell me I do that a lot."

"I'd say your friends are very astute." The look she shot him had a bit more spunk to it, and he straightened up again. He was surprised at how much he wanted to stay leaning close to her, looking into those multifaceted blue eyes.

"Well, they're also the ones who suggested I open a hot sauce shop, so you might want to reconsider your opinion of them," he said. "Look, it seems that you and I have things to talk about. Why don't you have dinner with me tonight?"

There was a flash of something he couldn't identify in her eyes. Distrust? Resentment? Dislike? No, he could swear it wasn't dislike. Still, she shook her head at his words.

"I can't," she said. "I have to celebrate the opening of my store."

"I'll join you," he said.

Hilary shook her head again. "No," she said firmly, wondering why she was so leery of connecting this attractive man with her own carefully planned life. Was it because of the way he'd made the ground tilt under her feet with his careless charm? "I have plans already."

"I see." He stroked his chin. Hilary could see the faint stubble along his jaw, and wondered if he, like herself, had gotten up at the crack of dawn this morning. "Dining with your family, are you?"

She knew what he was asking. "I'm not married, if that's what you mean," she said. "No, I'm having dinner with a colleague, and my two principal investors. We've been planning this for months.''

The thought of all her hard work and planning threatened to erase the unexpected pleasure she felt in Mac's company. Why couldn't he have turned up in her life in any other way?

"Tomorrow night, then," he said. "My treat."

Hilary stiffened her spine again. She hadn't wanted to complain about the financial hole she was in, and she wondered if that was the message he'd gotten. But he was leaning close to her again, disturbingly close, and she could swear there was no hint of patronage in his hazel eyes.

"After all," he said, the rasp gone from his voice now, "we really should talk."

"You're right," she murmured, already knowing this was going to be far from a business dinner. "Where and when?"

"I'll pick you up at your store," he said. "Fair's fair, you know. You've seen mine, now I want to see yours."

Hilary felt her breath quicken. The son of a gun was grinning again as he spoke, and she knew beyond any doubt that he'd intended the double meaning in his words. It was bad enough that he was here in the first place, and worse that he was laughing at her problems as though they didn't exist. But the suggestion that he found her attractive, or that he had noticed her attraction to him—that was something she couldn't allow to happen. She had too much at stake here.

His next words broke the spell. "What time do you close tomorrow?" he asked casually.

"We don't open on Sundays," she informed him. "In case you didn't know, Ottawa has a Sunday closing law—except in designated tourist areas like the Byward Market."

He had the grace to look uncomfortable. "Oh," he said. "Guess that gives me kind of an edge, doesn't it?"

"That, among other things," she said crisply. Her voice was cool now, almost formal. "I think it would be better if we just met at a restaurant. Do you have someplace in mind?''

He answered without missing a beat. "Domingo's, up on Bank Street," he said.

She recognized the name. Domingo's was the most popular of the new Ste. Helenean restaurants in Ottawa. "I take it your interest in hot sauce is more than just professional," she said.

"You bet." He flashed her that grin again. "And yours?"

She amazed herself by grinning back at him. "I never met a chili pepper I couldn't handle," she said. "My tolerance for the stuff is legendary in my family."

"Good. Just the kind of woman I like. The hotter the better—that's my motto."

"For women, or food?"

"Both."

Impudent, cocky, self-assured—there were a lot of appealing things about this man. And beneath the grin there was a sense of purpose that made Hilary want to know a lot more about him.

"Hot" was hardly how she'd have described herself, before this moment. But something in his smile, and the warmth of his hand on her shoulder as he showed her to the door, made her feel he'd turned on a hitherto unsuspected valve deep inside her. She could almost feel the steam heat hissing into every corner of her body.

The hotter the better, indeed, she thought. She was still savoring the sharp, salty taste of freedom on her tongue as she left the dark and disorganized little shop with the pirate in the doorway.

Two

Mac was uneasy.

It was a combination of several things. In the first place, it had been a long time since he'd had anything as formal as a dinner date with a woman he was attracted to. He'd found himself unsure about what he should wear, wondering whether he should ride his disreputable old motorcycle or make a better impression by taking a cab, whether she'd appreciate it if he brought her flowers. He'd settled on a plain white shirt with an open collar, tan trousers, the motorcycle and a single white rose.

In the second place, it was a long time since he'd felt this attracted to any woman. The jolt he'd felt at gut level the first time he looked into Hilary Gardiner's eyes was still with him as he waited for her in the restaurant.

It made him uneasy because she didn't fit in with any of his plans. He was in the middle of setting up the biggest and riskiest adventure of his admittedly adventurous career. And after that, he'd no doubt be posted to some corner of the world far from his hometown, as he had been for the past fifteen years. Beautiful dark-haired women with blue eyes like cut sapphires had no place in any of that.

In the third place, he was uneasy because he thought he'd spotted some men outside who had no business hanging around Domingo's. If they were who he thought they were, it behooved him to be extra watchful this evening.

He felt restless, turning in his chair, trying to find a comfortable position for his long legs. Sarah, the hostess, had given him the table he liked best, near the back and in a secluded corner.

"You look good tonight, Mac," she'd said, when he'd arrived.

"Thanks." He hadn't wanted to tell her about the men outside. If he was right, it was Sarah they were watching. Now, as he waited, he wondered if he would be wiser to put her on her guard.

All his uneasiness vanished when he saw Hilary walk in the front door. She looked like a tropical lily, he thought, rising to meet her. Her black hair shone like the velvet of night, and her skin was whiter than Caribbean sand.

"I must have had your complexion in mind when I picked this out," he said, handing her the single rose. Its creaminess contrasted with the deep electric blue of the pantsuit she wore, and perfectly matched the soft expanse of white skin at her throat, above her plunging V-neckline. "That color suits you, Hilary."

"Thank you." He liked her shy smile, and the faint flush that colored her fair skin at his compliment. "I figured if I was going to compete with a lot of Ste. Helenean red, I'd better wear something assertive."

Mac had grown so used to the ever-present reds of Ste. Helene that he barely noticed them. Now he glanced around the small restaurant, taking in Sarah's brilliant loose robe and the colorful costumes of the rest of the staff. The vibrant blue of Hilary's outfit was a good choice to stand up to their crimson surroundings, not to mention what it did for her dark, brilliant blue eyes.

"The lady has taste," he commented, as they both sat down. "And maybe some magical powers, as well."

"What do you mean?" That faint smile lingered, along with a slight wariness.

"I mean that with your hair pulled back like that, you look like a teenager. How do you do that? I could have sworn you told me you were thirty-two."

Hilary forced her smile upside down. "You're very charming, Mr. MacDougall," she told him, almost sternly. "I bet that glib tongue comes in handy for getting around Ste. Helenean export officials, doesn't it?"

"Oh, it comes in handy for all sorts of things," he said. "But in this case, it's absolutely sincere. I find you very attractive, Hilary Gardiner. And if you're going to have dinner with me, I insist that you call me Mac."

"All right, then. Mac."

Hilary had known this wouldn't be easy. All day long she'd had to keep reminding herself that she had business to discuss with this man—serious business. She couldn't simply treat their date as an evening out. But she'd suspected Mac would try to turn business into pleasure, and now, faced with his careless good looks across a very small table, she was finding it very hard to heed her own inner warning signals.

"Ever been here?" Mac was asking, as a waiter handed them two menus.

"No. I've just read the reviews. I don't actually eat out all that much."

Now, why had she admitted that? He was asking "Why not?" with a casual interest that implied he had a right to know.

She tapped a finger against the edge of the menu. "Partly because I love to cook," she said guardedly, "and partly—well, things have been pretty tight financially for me for a lot of years, and I guess I just got into the habit of not eating out.''

He was nodding at her, brows lowered. She was surprised at the sympathy in his hazel eyes.

"You haven't forgotten how it goes, have you?" he asked.

Hilary laughed. "I think it'll come back to me," she told him.

"Good. But just to be sure, why don't I start things off?"

From the way their waiter was hovering nearby, Hilary had a feeling Mac was an honored guest, not just another customer. He ordered drinks for both of them, and a round of appetizers.

"Sarah says you be sure to try the skewered goat," the waiter said.

"That sounds good. And don't forget the *poive* sauce. In fact..." Mac's eyes were gleaming now, with that unlawful laughter that made Hilary feel so unexpectedly good. "In fact, bring us out all the sauces you've got. Tell Sarah we've got a special guest tonight."

As the waiter moved away, Hilary leaned forward with her elbows on the table. "I get the feeling you're issuing a challenge," she said.

"Well, since you wouldn't show me your shop, I figured we'd do the next best thing, and have a tasting here."

She frowned again. "I didn't say I wouldn't show you my shop," she said. "I just said it wasn't open on Sundays."

The way he could arch one eyebrow and not the other was far too appealing. "Funny," he mused. "When we talked yesterday, I had the definite impression you didn't want me coming to *Fortissimo*."

Hilary racked her brains, trying to remember whether she'd even told him the name of her store. She concluded she hadn't. "Have you been checking up on me, Mac?" she demanded.

He chuckled, as though he'd scored a point. "In a minor way," he said. "I drove along Wellington Street this morning, before I opened up. That's a very attractive little setup you've got there.''

He was right, Hilary thought. She *didn't* want him intruding into her life, at least not yet. He was too much of an unknown, still too scary in that cavalier way of his.

"Thank you," she said coolly. "I worked hard to make it that way."

"I believe you." Watching her retreat behind that polite mask was like bait to Mac. He could feel himself rising to it. "Tell me, how did your celebration dinner go last night? Were your investors happy?"

"Very happy."

"I hope you went somewhere fancy."

Hilary hid a smile. "Actually we ordered out for pizza," she said.

"Must be pretty low-key investors."

She shook her head. "In some ways," she said. "In other ways, they can be pretty high-powered."

"And you don't want to talk about them."

"I didn't say that."

"No, but you get all cryptic whenever the subject comes up. You don't think I'm going to lure them away from you, do you?"

She couldn't hide her smile this time. "There's not a chance of that," she assured him.

"Then why so reluctant to talk about them—or about anything personal, for that matter?"

Why *was* she so reluctant? She couldn't put her finger on it. She only knew that some little voice inside her told her to be leery of letting this handsome pirate get too close before she knew more—a lot more—about him.

Their waiter had the good timing to bring their drinks and appetizers just then, and Hilary watched thankfully as Mac's attention turned to the more immediate subject of food. Even then, though, he kept probing her.

"Feeling brave?" he asked, lifting a plate in her direction. "These are baby squid—very tasty with *poive* sauce."

"When it comes to food, I'm probably braver than you think," she said, and proved it by taking a helping of squid on her own plate. She poured a generous dollop of the peppery island sauce on it, and ate it with enjoyment.

Mac lifted an eyebrow again, assessing her performance. "All right," he conceded, when he'd finished his own squid. "You're not just an amateur."

"Did you think I was?" The spicy flavors lingered on her tongue, making her whole mouth tingle.

For a moment Mac put down his fork and looked at her with unexpected seriousness. "I don't know what to think about you," he said. "I don't think I've ever met a woman like you."

"You mean, one who likes hot food?"

"Among other things." He shook his head, as if to clear away an unwelcome image, and Hilary found herself thinking again that his slightly curly dark brown hair always looked as though a sea breeze had just ruffled it. Then he proffered another plate, and she moved on to investigating the mysteries of skewered goat wrapped in banana leaves, with another in the array of hot sauces that had appeared on their small table.

By the time they'd finished dinner, even Hilary's capacity for stinging sauces was strained to the limits. "You must have signed an agreement with the devil," she said to Mac, watching him mop up the last drops of a sauce that was still making her ears burn. "Or were your taste buds permanently seared years ago?"

He grinned at her. "Nothing like that," he said. "It's just long years of practice, that's all. Do you have any idea how appealing you look with those flushed spots on your cheeks?"

Hilary pressed her hands to her face, and felt the warmth there. "You haven't even changed color," she said ruefully. "Well, that'll teach me to feel so cocky about my palate."

"Your palate is impressive," he assured her. "Most of my friends start calling the fire department after the first bite. With a few seasons in the islands, you'd be world-class."

Hilary took a sip of her beer, and looked surreptitiously at him. His strong hands were screwing the tops back on the assorted little bottles. There was such a careless grace in every move he made, as if he just knew that things would end up where he wanted them.

"How long did you live in the Caribbean?" she asked.

"About five years." The bottle he was dealing with seemed to demand his full attention suddenly.

"And you just got back a little while ago."

He looked up sharply. The glint in his eye reminded Hilary not to forget how purposeful he was, just beneath the surface. "Is that just a guess?" he said.

"More like a deduction. I never saw a landlocked Canadian with a tan like that before."

He glanced at his own strong brown hands, as if he'd rather they hadn't given him away. "You're right," he said. "I came back in April."

"Just after the coup in Ste. Helene." There was a breathless feeling in Hilary's midriff as she questioned him. He so obviously did not want to be questioned. "Is that where you were living?"

"Part of the time."

"And that's how you come to have connections who supply you with sauces I probably couldn't get if I proved I could walk on water," Hilary speculated out loud. "What were you doing on Ste. Helene in the first place, aside from working on your tan?"

It wasn't anger she could sense in him, but a deep determination not to satisfy her curiosity. Hilary didn't tolerate evasion nearly as well as she tolerated hot food, and she didn't want to hear him say what she suspected he was going to tell her.

"And don't just say 'This and that' again," she warned him. "I'm talking in specifics here."

He tapped a finger on the rim of his beer glass, looking speculatively at her. "I have no intention of telling you what I was doing down there," he said. "Is that specific enough?" And before she could quite recover from his sudden bluntness, he beat her to the draw and asked a question of his own. "What about you?" he said. "What did you do before you opened your store?"

Hilary leaned back in her chair. "I went to school," she said. "I just finished a business administration degree from the University of Ottawa."

"And before that?"

"Oh, Lord. I guess there *was* life before that, but I can barely remember it. It feels like I've been working on this degree forever."

"You weren't going to school full-time, then?"

"No." She felt the now-familiar caution about telling him too much, along with an unfamiliar need to unburden herself. "I couldn't afford to go full-time."

"So you were working, as well."

"Yes."

Mac was leaning forward now, eyes fastened on hers. He had the most likable eyes, she thought. Hazel and friendly and very, very perceptive.

"Doing what?"

"The university has a work/study program, for people returning to school. I was doing clerical work for them, as a way of earning my tuition and paying my expenses."

"I see." The two simple words told her he saw more than she intended him to. He saw, for instance, that she didn't want to be talking about herself any more than he had a moment ago.

"Look, Mac, I think we should get down to business," she said hurriedly, before he could dig any deeper. "After all, that *is* why we're here."

He gave an offhanded smile. "I'd almost forgotten that," he admitted. "I thought I was here because I like the food, and because I wanted to get to know you better."

"That's not the object of this meeting," she told him crisply. "We have a problem, you and I, and we need to figure out what to do about it."

"You mean, the problem of our two stores." He rubbed a hand along his jaw. Hilary was shocked to feel her fingertips tingling, as though she'd just shared that gesture with him and felt the faint raspiness of his cheekbone against her skin.

"Of course that's what I mean." How could the man be so casual about this? He must be wading in money, she thought, even though that didn't fit with all her other impressions of him. "I've done a lot of projections on my store. If I can't break even this first year, I'll be down the tubes. And with you sitting down there in the market happily selling Ste. Helenean goodies to every buyer in town, breaking even for me looks like more and more of a pipe dream."

"Look at it this way. Once I'm gone, you'll have all the buyers to yourself."

"*If* I survive that long. Mac, you don't seem to understand how far out on a limb I am on this thing. If I'd had any sense at all, I probably would have turned my business degree into some nice, secure job with a multinational corporation."

"Why didn't you?"

She shrugged, echoing his own characteristic gesture. "I've always wanted to run my own business," she said. "One of the reasons I worked so hard on that degree was so I could be my own boss someday. And now I finally am, and the first thing that happens is you come along to threaten to take it all away from me." She couldn't help the slight edge of panic in her tone.

He was frowning at her now, sympathetic but not desperately concerned. "What's the worst-case scenario?" he asked. "You end up paying off a bank loan, right?"

"Wrong. I don't have a bank loan. I wanted to keep complete control of this business from the beginning, so I used my own savings. And if things don't work out, I'm in deep trouble. No retirement fund, no financial cushion to fall back on, no university education for my sons—"

She stopped. She hadn't meant to get that far. It was as though telling him about her boys was the first step in a long line of admissions she didn't want to make to this man.

And he hadn't missed it. "Your what?" he said slowly.

"My two sons. That's who I meant when I mentioned my investors. It's principally their university funds that I used to get *Fortissimo* going."

Mac had had a sense all along that there was much more to Hilary than met the eye. Her reluctant admission just proved it to him.

"They must be far too young to have any say in the matter," he prompted.

"They're fourteen." She could see him doing the arithmetic in his head, the way people always did when they found out she was the mother of two strapping adolescents, who were almost men. "Yes I was a child bride. Go ahead and say it."

"Did you plan to be a child mother, too?"

Well, she'd give him credit for getting right to the point—not that she was about to answer the question.

"We're way off the track here, Mac," she said firmly. "My personal life has nothing to do with our situation, except to make it clear why it's so important to me to have *Fortissimo* succeed. The question is—"

Their waiter glided up to the table again, removing their plates and telling Mac that Sarah thought they might like to have their dessert and coffee in the side garden. "It's a nice night," he added.

"Good point. We'll do that."

"Mac, you're not listening. We haven't even started to talk about the problem yet."

He stood, stretching his long legs and holding out a hand to her side of the table. "You heard the man," he said. "It's a nice night. On Ste. Helene, enjoying the weather is much more important than discussing business."

Hilary stayed stubbornly where she was, resisting the lure of that outstretched hand. She felt herself wanting to reach out to it, to have Mac pull her to her feet and up toward him. And at the same time she was afraid of where that might lead.

"If enjoying the weather is so important on Ste. Helene, it's a wonder anyone gets anything done," she muttered.

Mac only grinned. "The important things get done," he assured her, and from the rakish tilt of that grin, she had a feeling what some of those things were. She had a sudden vision of two sun-warmed bodies lying on the golden sand, oblivious to the surf gliding around them.

Her own imagination seemed to be on Mac's side. Hilary cleared her throat, trying to get back to real life. "How about business?" she demanded. "Does that get done, too?"

"Sooner or later. And just at the moment, I'd prefer to make it later. Come on." The man wasn't going to take no for an answer, she realized, and slowly, she reached for his hand. "Domingo's banana pie will put the world of business in the proper perspective for you."

Hilary couldn't remember feeling this split in half by anyone. On the one hand, he was driving her crazy with his casual refusal to treat their problem seriously. Clearly his whole existence was run on the same principles as his shop: open when you feel like it, close when you're tired of being open, do everything else when you get to it. It went contrary to everything she knew.

On the other hand, she honestly couldn't remember feeling so light-headed simply because an attractive man was holding her hand. He was pulling her along, threading his way between the small tables and out the front door, and Hilary felt an unexpected and very pleasant buoyancy in her legs as she followed.

He tugged in too many directions at once, and she found herself simply wanting to let go and follow where he led. It wasn't like her.

She'd noticed the gate to the side garden when she'd arrived. Mac headed in that direction, and Hilary was taking in a deep breath, enjoying the warmth of the summer night and the closeness of her handsome buccaneer, when she became aware of a change in him.

He slowed, tightening his grip on her hand. She could feel him tensing, as if he were waiting for something, and she heard him mutter something under his breath.

"What did you say?" she asked quietly, as though his sudden wariness was catching.

He looked down at her. "Just that I've been letting an evening with a beautiful lady distract me from something I should have remembered." He paused, hesitated, and then seemed to come to a decision. "Look, Hilary, I need you to do me a favor. It's an easy one, and there's no way it could be dangerous, but it's important to me, okay?"

The word *dangerous* hopped out at her. In spite of Mac's assurances, something whispered to Hilary, *See? He is a pirate, after all.*

"What's the favor?" she asked guardedly.

"I'm going to take the back way around to the garden. But I want you to go out the front, and through the side gate, near where you came in. And I want you to watch—as casually as you can—for two guys in a maroon Buick. They're probably sitting up at the corner directly ahead of you, but they may be somewhere else by now. Just sort of glance over the street, and see if you can spot them.''

They were standing in the small vestibule, and Mac was still holding her hand. She could feel the persuasion in the warmth of his touch.

''Do I get to ask why I'm doing this?''

He sighed. She could see frustration in his eyes. ''There's no reason for you to be bothered with it,'' he said. ''Just trust me that there's no risk involved, and that it'll help me out a lot.''

She looked even more deeply into his hazel eyes, and knew she didn't trust him. And why should she, when he'd started sounding like something out of a spy movie all of a sudden? He was, after all, nearly a stranger.

No, he wasn't. He tightened his grip on her hand suddenly, and she found herself gripping him in return. There was something between them already that made her feel they'd never been strangers. That little buzz she felt when he looked at her proved it.

''All right,'' she said finally. ''A maroon Buick, you said?''

She knew she was far too susceptible to that sudden, flashing grin of his. It was reckless, brash, all the things she was so careful not to allow herself to be. It was also sexier than any mere grin had a right to be.

She waited until she saw him leave the restaurant through the kitchen exit, and then stepped outside. She was barely aware of the warmth of the night air, or the few strolling passersby. It was hard work to look casual when you really weren't, she discovered. But she managed to survey the street without seeming to, noting that there *was* a maroon Buick with two men in it parked at the next corner.

She passed on that news to Mac when she met him inside the walled garden. ''They were just sitting there,'' she reported. ''Like they were waiting for someone.''

It occurred to her, the moment the words were out of her mouth, that they must *be* waiting for someone. Suddenly the two anonymous men took on a threatening aspect. Was it Mac they were waiting for?

"Mac," she said quickly, "what's going on?"

He waved her question aside. His face seemed older now, and tougher, no longer the laughing pirate but the hardened sea captain. Somehow, she'd suspected this side of him was there. It was one of the things that had made her so wary of him.

"Stay here," he said curtly. "I'll be right back."

It was issued as an order. He ducked back into the restaurant through the kitchen door, while Hilary stood there with a myriad of elaborate plots shaping themselves in her head. She didn't like the feeling that Mac was mixed up in something that might be dangerous—and from the look in his eye, she knew it might be, no matter what he'd said to the contrary. And even more, she didn't like the way she'd suddenly ceased to exist for him. His undivided attention, earlier this evening, had been a very seductive thing.

She was still trying to sort things out when he returned. "Sorry," he said brusquely. "I had to make a quick call."

"Mac," she said, "who are those two guys out there?"

"I don't know, exactly."

"But you obviously have some idea."

Mac sighed and ran a hand along his jaw. "It's nothing you need to worry about," he told her. "But if it makes you feel any better, the call I just made was to the police. I reported a couple of suspicious characters loitering outside, and asked if they could be moved along. With any luck, that'll take care of the problem."

She knew that wasn't the whole story. Mac was heading for the front gate of the garden now, obviously being careful not to show himself in the open doorway. Hilary followed, against her better judgment.

"What *is* the problem?" she demanded. "Why are you being so mysterious all of a sudden?"

He wasn't listening to her. Once again, she found herself missing the attentive man who'd listened so carefully earlier in the evening. This tense stranger was making her very nervous.

Well, she didn't want to be a part of whatever he was mixed up in. Burying her regret at the way their evening had turned out, Hilary stood up as straight as she could, and said, "It looks like you've got enough to keep you occupied for the rest of the evening, Mac. I guess I'll be going now."

She started for the open gate, but before she could reach it, he took hold of her with both hands, and pulled her toward him.

"Not yet," he said tersely.

She was close enough to him that she could feel the warmth of his skin through his open-collared white shirt. "What do you mean not yet?" she said. "Look, Mac, either you answer some of my questions, or I'm out of here."

It was useless to push against him. He was simply too strong. But she tried anyway, because it was maddening to feel that she'd somehow wandered into his intrigue and couldn't get out again.

The only other diners in the garden were at the far side of the patio, and completely engrossed in their own conversation. Hilary pulled away first in one direction and then the other, and the only result was that Mac held her tighter, and by the time she stopped struggling, he held her against his side with an arm that was as strong as a vise.

"I'm sorry." His voice was very close to her ear. Some of the hard edge was gone now, and the sound of it gave her an unexpected pulsing thrill inside. "But they might have seen you, just now. If you come right back out again, they may suspect something's up. Just wait a couple of minutes, until the police show up."

Waiting a couple of minutes, clamped against Mac in this intimate way, promised to be both an ordeal and a treat, Hilary thought. She was confusedly aware of her own body's response to his nearness. His arm, rock-hard and unyielding, was crushed against her breasts, and the sensation was doing some wild things to her equilibrium.

"Um . . . How about loosening up a little?" she managed to say. She was trying to sound casual, but she didn't manage it. Her voice was breathy, with the echo of her heightened heartbeat in it.

Mac was fighting himself, silently, and losing. Damn it, he was enjoying holding her like this. Her curves fit perfectly against him, the lush swell of her hip cradled by his thighs. Deep inside he felt the stirrings of an unmistakable desire, and he shifted his grasp slightly. With any luck, she'd think he was just holding her tighter, and not realize he was really trying to hide the evidence of his physical response to her.

It didn't work. He was certain she could feel his arousal through that lightweight blue pantsuit, certain she knew how much he suddenly wanted to move more seductively against her. Mac cleared his throat.

"Forget it," he said, trying to sound brusque past the sudden huskiness in his voice. "And have you running out there and tipping those guys off? No way."

The way she squirmed against him in protest was headily erotic. Mac almost groaned, feeling his response to her growing. In two seconds he was going to forget all about the silent surveillance outside, and turn this unexpected embrace into something much more.

She smelled like violets. Her shiny black hair was brushing against his cheek, and the scent of it swam in his senses, hypnotizing him. "Damn," he said, involuntarily. "Do you have any idea what you do to me, Hilary Gardiner?"

The words were out before he even realized he was speaking. He felt her stop moving suddenly, and then turn slowly in his grip until she could see his face.

Her lips were slightly parted, kissable, inviting. The faint peach gloss on them only enhanced her own fair coloring, making her seem like an alabaster statue come suddenly to life. He had had that feeling about her from the first: that she'd been waiting for something, or someone, to make her hidden fantasies flower into full, living color.

She'd been waiting for him, he thought confusedly. He was sure of it.

And one kiss would prove it. For the moment, the restaurant garden and the sounds of the street outside didn't exist. Only Hilary, and the questioning look in her multifaceted blue eyes, mattered to Mac.

"This is crazy," she breathed.

"I couldn't agree more." He lowered his head then, brushing her lips with his own. His mind was flooded by the foreknowledge of the sweetness within her, the hidden springs he wanted to taste. The faint scent of violets surrounded him as he closed his eyes to the everyday world and prepared to lose himself in Hilary Gardiner.

The police chose that moment to show up. Of course it would turn out that way, Mac thought as the sound of official walkie-talkies and the idling of a car outside the restaurant intruded his consciousness.

"Damn," he muttered, against Hilary's hair.

Her large blue eyes were filled with questions now. And he couldn't answer any of them for her. It was wiser not to try to get involved at all, he knew. He couldn't possibly be what a woman like Hilary needed. It was just that when he held her in his arms...

He'd lost control of the rational part of his brain. Therefore, it would be better not to take her in his arms again, and avoid temptation altogether. With a reluctance that was like a physical pain, Mac loosened his grip and stepped away from her.

Hilary felt as though she'd been submerged in a warm sea and had just shot to the surface. The sensation left her gasping for air, and made her heart thud against her rib cage.

What had just happened? For an instant she'd lost track of everything, of their surroundings, of the threat Mac represented to her, of *Fortissimo,* of whatever crazy mystery he was tangled up in. For an instant she was ready to give herself to him gladly. She'd been eager—no, make that hungry—for the taste of his mouth on hers, for the intriguing world of desire and fulfillment she'd glimpsed in his eyes when she'd turned to face him.

And now, just as suddenly, he'd withdrawn from her. His attention was completely focused on the squad car outside, and the two uniformed policemen who were walking slowly toward the maroon Buick.

Hilary forced herself to pay attention to the little drama unfolding on the sidewalk. Anything was better than trying to unravel the complicated mix of feelings Mac had plunged her into this evening.

The officers knocked on the Buick's window, and the driver slowly rolled it down. She could see the two men more clearly now. The driver was black, his companion white. Both looked stonily uninterested in what the policeman was saying to them.

Beside her, Mac was muttering under his breath again. "Don't give them a chance to run," she heard him say. "Be ready for them."

The officer was gesturing toward the restaurant now, as if telling the men they couldn't loiter there any longer. Hilary was still close enough to Mac that she could feel the tension building in him again, and hear his breath coming more shallowly.

"They're going to take off," he predicted. "And those cops aren't ready."

"What can you do about it?" she asked him.

He didn't answer. She saw the change in that athletic body of his, from languid lover to pirate on the high seas again. She felt him poise to move, waiting to see which way things went.

They went with a squeal and a roar, as the maroon Buick shot out from under the policeman's warning hand. The big car careened down Bank Street, and was a block away, ignoring a red light, before the officers had reacted and headed for their own car.

Mac was right behind them. Hilary had noticed a beat-up looking motorcycle parked by the front door when she'd first arrived. Something about its loud purple gas tank and the rakish angle it was leaning at had reminded her fleetingly of Mac.

It turned out she'd been right. In record time he sprinted across the sidewalk and launched himself onto the old bike, kicking it into life with a resounding roar. With a spare five seconds to slam a helmet on his head, and no time at all to acknowledge that she was still standing there watching him, he spun away from the curb, passed the police car at the first cross street and tore off into the night.

It took perhaps another half minute before it occurred to Hilary that she wasn't breathing. She exhaled the breath she'd been holding, shakily, and was hauling in another one when she became aware of someone standing next to her.

It was Sarah. And as she focused more clearly on the tall, red-clad hostess, Hilary realized that it was the same woman she'd seen coming out of Mac's shop yesterday.

"That Mac, he sure does know how to go someplace in a hurry," Sarah was saying, her softly accented voice as attractive as the rest of her.

"You can say that again," Hilary said. "I feel like I've been left behind in a cloud of dust."

Sarah's soft laugh did something to ease the tension Hilary was feeling. "You Mac's date?" she drawled.

Hilary nodded.

"Too bad he ran out on you like this."

"Does he do this often?"

"Run out on ladies? Or date them in the first place?"

Hilary had been referring to the running out, not the dating, but suddenly she was curious to know more about the mysterious John Augustus Laurier MacDougall. And she had a feeling there was a lot Sarah could tell her. "Both," she said finally.

Sarah smiled broadly. "He's a loner, that Mac," she told Hilary. "I never see him here with a woman before. And I never see him move that fast, either." Her smile faded, and Hilary saw a look of worry in her face that somehow mirrored Mac's own expression not too long ago.

"What is this all about?" she couldn't help asking.

"Did Mac tell you?"

"Not a thing."

Sarah shook her head, heavy earrings swaying slightly. "Then it's better I don't, either," she said.

Hilary shook her own head, echoing Sarah's gesture. She couldn't believe, at this stage of her life when she'd finally gotten some measure of control over her own destiny, that she'd somehow become involved with an honest-to-goodness buccaneer.

"Well, I think I'm not going to wait for him," she said, surprised at the little nagging worry for Mac that was filling her chest. "If he comes back—"

"Oh, he'll come back," Sarah said with assurance. "Mac always comes back."

Hilary wasn't at all surprised to hear it. "Just tell him I had to leave, would you?" she asked. "Tell him—tell him when he said we were going to have a spicy meal, I thought he was just referring to the food."

Sarah's smile came back full force, and the sympathy in it made Hilary feel a little better as she headed for her car, and home.

Three

—

"C'mon, Mom." Todd wasn't about to take no for an answer. "This was the first date you've gone on in ages, and you won't even tell us about it?"

"No fair," Andrew echoed from *Fortissimo*'s back room.

Hilary sighed. "There's really not much to tell," she hedged. "And anyway, when you guys went to the junior prom this year, did I pump you for details?"

"Yes," they chorused.

She sighed again. "Well, that's only because I'm your mother. I'm supposed to know what you're up to."

"We're just returning the favor," Andrew pointed out reasonably. "You look out for us, we look out for you, right?"

Hilary knew it was right. She'd been so young when her boys were born—young and not very wordly-wise—that sometimes she felt as though the three of them had all grown up together.

Todd was nodding his dark head energetically, confirming his brother's words. "So spill," he said. "What's the guy look like?"

After some hard thought in the small hours of the morning, Hilary had come to a decision. Since Mac had so noisily roared out of her life last night, she had a strong feeling it would be wisest just to keep him out of it. She'd figure a way around the problem of their competing stores on her own. In the meantime, she supposed there wasn't any harm in describing the man to her sons.

"Tall," she said, and instantly the image of his rangy, long-legged form swam into her mind. "Brown hair, a little bit curly." *Ruffled by a breath of air from the sea.* "Hazel eyes. Nice eyes." She couldn't help admitting that. "Not much on fancy dress. Prefers jeans, I'd say. Quite a good-looking guy."

"Drives an old motorcycle," Todd supplied.

Hilary nodded, then tensed. "Who on earth told you that?" she demanded.

"Just a lucky guess. 'Cause there's a guy like you just described getting off an old motorcycle in front of our door."

"Oh, wow," Andrew said, coming out of the back room to see. "That's a Triumph."

"Jeez, you're right."

And then both boys were out of the shop and heading for the sidewalk, leaving Hilary inside with a suddenly pounding heart and a feeling of mingled anger and relief that he hadn't, after all, just vanished last night.

Carefully, she put down the bottle of hot sauce she'd been holding. Mac had some explaining to do, and she wasn't going to let him storm in here and charm her half to death the way he'd done last night. Last night...

She caught her breath with the memory of the things she'd felt caught in Mac's arms, pressed so sensuously against his body. No free-roving pirate should have the power to make her feel so giddy, so poundingly alive.

And she wasn't going to give him that power again. She straightened her spine, drawing herself up to her full height, and watched as Mac disentangled himself from the boys' excited motorcycle questions and headed inside.

Todd and Andrew stayed with the bike. Hilary was alone with her pirate in the small shop, and once again, as she had every time she'd seen him, she didn't know whether to stay or run.

She stayed, standing tall beside the glass-topped counter. Mac was grinning at her, and the crinkled laugh lines at the sides of his eyes made him look closer to the thirty-seven years he'd admitted to last night.

"Sarah gave me your message," he said. He leaned against the door frame as he spoke, as though he had the sense to be a little unsure of his welcome.

"I see you got back in one piece." It was ridiculous to feel so shaky inside, just because a handsome man with perceptive, laughing eyes was looking at you that way. It was even more ridiculous to feel so relieved that he *had* gotten back in one piece.

"Oh, sure. The old bike makes a lot of noise, but it always gets me where I'm going."

"I wasn't thinking about the bike," Hilary admitted. "I was thinking about the guys you were following." When he didn't answer right away, she added, "Did you catch them?"

He laughed. "I wasn't trying to catch them," he said. "I just wanted to see where they went. I managed to do that, and the rest is up to the police."

"Mac, what was—"

He held up a hand. "I didn't come here to talk about them," he said firmly. "I came to see if I could talk you into another dinner out with me, without the bad guys, this time."

Hilary folded her arms across her chest, protectively. This was going to take a lot of willpower...maybe more than she had.

"I'd like to see you again," she said, sounding calmer than she felt. "But first I need to clear up what happened last night. I'm not used to finding myself in the middle of detective mysteries, Mac."

"You won't find yourself in the middle of another one," he said, quickly. "I'm sorry for getting you mixed up in that whole business last night. I should have just taken care of it myself."

He seemed annoyed as he spoke. She wondered if it was himself, or her, or the whole situation, that he was mad at.

"That's not what I mean," she said. "You can't just pretend last night never happened." How could she explain herself to a man who leaped on ratty old motorcycles and went tearing off after mysterious characters as if he were the Lone Ranger?

"As far as we're concerned, it didn't happen," he said stubbornly.

Outside, the boys seemed to be wrapping up their inspection of Mac's bike. Hilary spoke quickly, wanting to get this said before her sons came back in.

"Mac, try to understand," she said. "I lead a pretty low-key life. I have my family, my home, now my business. I have enough money to get by on—just—and enough time to spend with the people I love. And I've worked darn hard to get to that stage."

"I can see that." His lowered brows made her wonder if he really did see.

"The point is that for a long time I was scrambling. I made a couple of bad mistakes early on—"

"What mistakes?"

She didn't care to go into detail. "Things I could easily have avoided," she said. "Things that meant that for years and years I had a tough time. And now that I've gotten past all that, I'm not crazy about jumping into strange situations and taking chances again.''

"You think I'm a chance you don't want to take?''

She looked at him, in his well-worn jeans and T-shirt—blue today—and his rakish grin and aggressively male stance, and said, "Yes. That's exactly what I think.''

Mac glanced over his shoulder, as if aware that they might be joined by the boys at any moment. "What were the mistakes you made?'' he asked her. "Were they chances you took, that didn't work out?''

"I guess you could put it that way.''

"Why don't you like talking about this?''

"Probably for the same reason you don't want to let me know what was going on last night,'' she said. "It's a private part of me, something I'm not comfortable sharing.''

He didn't take the hint. "How old were you when you got married?'' he wanted to know.

Hilary frowned at him. "Seventeen,'' she said.

"And the boys were born the next year?''

"Yes.''

"Were they planned?''

She felt a flush starting on her cheeks. "I don't want to get into this, Mac,'' she said firmly.

Her firmness made no impression. But the fact that Todd and Andrew were coming back into the store did. "I want to know all about this, Hilary,'' Mac said quickly. "I want to know everything about you. I want to know why you're so leery of me. Damn it—'' He tried to bite off the next words, but they spilled out anyway. "I want to know why I can't stop thinking about the way you felt next to me last night. I want to know that most of all.''

She'd barely had time to catch her breath at the passion that surfaced in his voice when the boys came in. The cheery sound of the bells on the door were crazily out of place in the highly-charged atmosphere of the little shop.

"I'm going to get a bike as soon as I'm out of school," Todd said, without preamble.

"You most certainly are not," Hilary told him. "Even your father admits now how dangerous motorcycles can be."

Todd turned to Mac, grinning, and said, "My dad used to have this great old Harley. He says Mom never did like it."

"Is that so?" Mac raised an eyebrow.

Hilary felt her fingers curling into frustrated fists. Mac had waltzed in here ten minutes ago, and already her own son was addressing him as man-to-man, leaving her out of it. It was too much.

"My main objection to that bike was that Skip cared more about it than he did about his family," she said, squashing the bad memories that came with her words. It was to her credit, she thought, that she didn't come right out and say that Skip had walked out on the three of them principally because he preferred his vehicles and his free-and-easy life-style to the responsibilities of raising the family he'd started.

Now it was Andrew who was being buddy-buddy with Mac, interpreting his mother's last statement.

"My dad left us when we were three," he explained. "I guess she told you about that."

"As a matter of fact, she's been reticent on the whole subject," Mac said. Damn the man, he was enjoying this! The angrier she got, the more pronounced Mac's grin was becoming.

"It's not like I'm the only one being reticent," she shot back, feeling her temper start to get the better of her. She saw the boys' surprised glances. They knew it took a lot to make her mad, and they obviously couldn't figure out how Mac had managed to do it so quickly.

"What do you mean?" Todd asked her.

"I mean that Mac has a few secrets of his own," she said.

"Yeah?" The boys looked at Mac, considering this new angle.

Her direct words had finally wiped out that disconcerting grin. "They're not my secrets," he said neutrally. "Other people are involved. I can't just spill the beans to whoever I want."

"That's fine. But don't expect you can just open me up like a tin can, either."

She wasn't sure why she was being so adamant about this. She felt unexpectedly like a mother hen, standing there with her chicks and watching a fox walk into their midst.

Todd and Andrew weren't missing the tension in her tone. They looked at each other, and then at their mother. "We're going to head home now, okay?" Andrew said, speaking for the two of them as he often did. "See you there."

"Maybe we'll take a rain check on that ride you promised," Todd added, to Mac.

Mac's sidelong glance told Hilary he knew he'd stepped in it. "If your mother thinks it's all right," he said quickly.

Hilary said nothing. He was a fast worker, all right: within minutes, he'd recruited the boys by offering something no red-blooded teen was going to turn down.

When they'd gone, she steeled herself to put an end to this impossible situation. "Mac, listen to me," she said.

He started to speak, but she cut in on top of his words. "Just listen," she repeated. "And don't try to get past me with that charming tongue of yours, because this time I'm sure of what I want to say, and you need to hear it."

She paused, and he said, "All right, let's have it."

He could see her gathering in a deep breath. She was fighting her attraction to him, he thought, and something in the tilt of her chin told him she believed she was winning. Well, he'd see about that.

"There's no sense pursuing this," she began.

"Too late," he said. He made himself sound as jaunty as he knew how. "You've got your store open, and I've got mine. How can we not pursue it?"

"That wasn't what I meant, and you know it."

"What did you mean, then?" He was pushing her deliberately, wanting to hear her admit that they'd already moved on well past a simple business relationship.

"You're being difficult, Mac."

"It's one of the things I do best." He gave her his widest grin.

"Could you be serious for two minutes, and listen to what I'm trying to say?"

"Sure, if you'll make it a little clearer for me. You said there's no sense pursuing 'this.' I'm just trying to find out what you think 'this' is."

He could see the pulse beat at the soft white center of her collarbone. He felt his whole body tighten as he watched that steady rhythm pick up speed. She was breathing faster, he realized. Just as he was.

" 'This' means you and me," she said.

There was a sudden silence in the little shop, a silence packed with unspoken and very settling words. She'd admitted it, Mac thought. She'd taken what must have been a giant step for someone as cautious as she was, and acknowledged that there was such a thing as "you and me" between them. The idea of it filled him with something like wonder.

Unfortunately, she was taking quick action to cancel out the hidden promise of the words she'd just said. "We would have been far smarter just to keep this on a professional basis," she was telling him now.

Mac shook his head adamantly. He felt his hair curling down over his forehead, as it always did no matter how hard he tried to brush it back. He wanted to feel Hilary's gentle fingers tangled in it, he thought fiercely. He wanted to know how she felt, how she tasted, how she would touch him.

Most of all, he wanted to know what was beneath those layers of ingrained caution. He had a feeling it would be enough to change a man's world-view in the single blink of an eye.

"It's too late for that, too," he said. "We left business behind the moment we touched each other, last night. You know it's true, Hilary."

There was a touch of desperation in the kaleidoscopic blue of her eyes now. "You're not listening," she said. "There's no place in my life for a man like you, and I suspect there's not much room for me in yours."

That was entirely too accurate, and Mac knew it. He felt his jaw tighten. "Just because I ran out on you on our first date?" he demanded.

"No, not just because of that. It's—it's just something about you. You're too reckless for me. You're not what I want."

Her wide-open blue eyes told him she was struggling to believe it herself. "Too reckless," he echoed.

"You know you are. If the same situation came up again, you know you'd jump on that old bike and take off in just the same way. And I'm not comfortable being left on the sidewalk, knowing there's a mystery out there."

"So you want to be let in on the mystery."

"I want there not to *be* a mystery." That was the heart of the matter, and Hilary's voice quivered a little as she spoke. "I want things on an even keel, Mac. I've had too many years of trying to keep everything together. I want peace and quiet, not crazy motorcycle chases."

She was absolutely right. There was no way a rover like himself could ever fit into her safe, comfortable life. And, he reminded himself, no way a woman like Hilary could drop everything and join him on his globe-hopping adventures. They just weren't cut out for each other.

The hell of it was that he knew she was right, and he still couldn't help wanting her. And if he was any judge at all, she wanted him just as fiercely. He hadn't just imagined her response to the kiss that had almost happened last night.

He had to know. He had to make sure he wasn't just dreaming this, and more than anything, he had to drink in the sweetness he'd only just tasted when his lips had brushed hers yesterday. Smothering something like a growl, he closed the distance between them in the little shop, and pulled her toward him again.

"Stop it, Mac," she was saying, eyes very wide now. "You're just doing this because you can't think of anything to prove me wrong."

She was right, but he wasn't about to admit it. "I'll prove you wrong," he said thickly. "You know there's something between us, Hilary—something that has nothing to do with hot sauce or security or motorcycle chases or anything except just being a man and a woman who want each other."

"I never said—" Her words came out on a gasp as their bodies met. "I never said I want you."

The last three words were all Mac heard. She said them with a kind of desperation that went straight to his head, and then spread with a pleasurable pang to several other places that had been longing inescapably for Hilary ever since he'd met her.

"I want you, too," he muttered. He felt her straining against him, felt all her fears and frustrations for an instant as she tried to resist what both of them were feeling.

And then in another instant he felt it all melt away, and instead of pulling back she was moving willingly toward him, meeting his lips, seeking his kiss, answering his hungry moan by opening her mouth and letting him into the hidden softness he'd been dreaming about.

"Oh, God." The words were ground out against her mouth. Mac's whole frame was tight with need, crushing her against him. Was he hurting her? From the little whimper deep in her throat, he almost thought he must be. Then he recognized the passion in the sound, and it almost drove him over the edge.

"Hilary." Dragging his lips from hers took an almost superhuman effort. "Don't tell me we're not right together. Not when it feels this good."

The moment he'd spoken, he knew he'd made a mistake. Hilary took in a long breath, and then pulled back, turning half away from him.

"It's still a mistake," she said shakily. "And you know it is."

He should have held on to her, he thought crazily. He should have let the pulsing need he could feel in both of them just take over, until it had convinced her.

Convinced her of what? The sobering thought slowed down Mac's racing imagination. Convinced her to go to bed with him? Even Mac, for all his recklessness, had never been a man to go hopping into bed with women he'd only just met. Convinced her to see him again? She'd made her objections to that perfectly clear, and he knew they still held water.

"All I know," he said raggedly, "is that I never felt the way I feel when I'm near you. And I have a sneaking suspicion it's the same for you. And when two people feel that way about each other, I think it's crazy to throw it away."

She looked up, as if there might be an escape route in the ceiling. She didn't find one, and finally she turned to face him. "Those are easy words to say, Mac," she said, and he caught the regret in her tone. "But they're not easy to act on, and believe me, I'm speaking from experience."

"That damned juvenile you married, you mean." What had she called him? Biff? No, Skip. He couldn't imagine a woman of Hilary's grace and elegance marrying anybody named Skip.

Her chin came up, as if he'd challenged her. "I loved him," she said forcefully. "I thought he was the whole world, back then. And I—well, I was wrong. But by the time

I found that out, I was already locked in a situation I couldn't get out of."

"Because you got pregnant by mistake." His frustration was making him sound too blunt, he knew. But *something* had to crack that shell she was using to defend her feelings with.

Her eyes flashed at him, a hundred different shades of blue. "My boys were not a mistake," she said angrily.

"That wasn't what I meant," he began, but she didn't let him finish.

"Raising my sons is the most important thing I've ever done," she said.

"And you've obviously done a good job."

She tossed her head. "I'm not interested in your approval rating," she said. "What I meant was, having children when I did taught me a hard lesson. I plan things now. I don't let them just happen. I don't give in to sudden impulses, the way you did just now."

"The way *I* did?" The woman could be maddening. Mac felt his own hot temper starting to fizzle. "I could have sworn there was a little reciprocal feeling in that kiss, lady."

"For the last time, Mac, that was a mistake. This whole thing is just wrong. Trust me."

"I don't think you trust yourself. That's why you want to get rid of me so badly."

She folded her arms again. More protective armor, he thought. "If I don't trust myself, that's my problem," she said coolly. "It's five o'clock, Mac, and I'd like to close up the shop. Would you leave now, please?"

"With pleasure." He needed to get away, to clear his head and figure out just what Hilary Gardiner did to him and why. "But don't think you've seen the last of me."

"Anytime you want to come in and buy some hot sauce, I'll be glad to see you," she said with deceptive sweetness, and opened the door for him. As he left, she flipped over the sign that hung there. When Mac glanced back on his way to his bike, he could still see her blue eyes, right next to the sign that said CLOSED in no uncertain terms.

Her house was exactly what Mac had expected.

He'd grown up on the diplomatic, establishment side of the nation's capital, surrounded by big old homes and spacious gardens. Hilary's neighborhood, with its small houses and pocket-size lawns, was a part of Ottawa he'd never been familiar with. But as soon as he found her address, it was easy to equate the trim, well-kept house with the need for security and stability she'd talked about on Monday. From the neat gray stucco to the prolifically flowering bushes on the lawn, the place spoke of care and attention to the many details of domestic life.

His beat-up Triumph motorcycle looked like a renegade, parked behind Hilary's little sedan.

Mac sighed, and pulled the rolled-up magazine out of his back pocket. He stuffed it under his arm, and climbed her front steps. He hoped he was doing the right thing. The hell of it was, he didn't seem to be able to do anything else.

She answered the door in her bathrobe. It was a light blue summer-weight robe, and left an appealing stretch of very shapely leg clearly in view.

"Hi," he said, trying to sound offhanded. It didn't quite work. He was, as always, too stirred up by the simple sight of her, and he knew it was apparent in the sound of his voice.

"Hello." Her answer was tentative. "Do you have any idea what time it is?"

He glanced at his watch, and cleared his throat. "I guess it's a little on the early side, isn't it?" he said. "I wanted to see you before—that is, assuming you get the Sunday paper—can I come in?"

He ended the unsuccessful sentence with a lopsided grin. She hesitated for a long moment, and then opened the door.

"The boys are still sleeping," she said. "They're not morning people, as the saying goes."

"I never knew a teenage boy who was," Mac said, stepping into her kitchen. "At least, I sure wasn't. My mother used to have to come into my room shaking half a dozen ice cubes in a bucket to get me out of bed."

She actually smiled at that. "Did she ever actually use them?" she asked.

"Only once." Mac sat down at the table without waiting for an invitation. He had a feeling that the more ensconced he got, the harder it would be for her to throw him out when she found out why he'd come. "It was just after I'd gotten my bike. I was seventeen. I'd been out kind of late, riding around, and I was dead to the world. The first thing I knew there were ice cubes skating around under my covers, and my mother was laughing at me from the doorway."

"Sounds as though she knew how to deal with teenagers," Hilary commented. "So you've had that bike forever?"

She still didn't sound wild about the Triumph. Mac tempered his own enthusiasm for the old bike by saying, "Well, it was in storage for a long time. I used it while I was going to university, but it's been in my parents' garage for a lot of years. It's only since I've been back in Ottawa that I've been riding it again."

"And are you back for good?"

Hilary moved to the coffeemaker while she asked the question, and poured out two cups of freshly made coffee. When she'd seen Mac's tousled brown hair and laughing eyes on the other side of her screen door five minutes ago, her first impulse had been to tell him to go away. But then he'd grinned at her, and she'd gone all weak in the knees, and now, as she handed him a mug full of steaming coffee, she felt herself giving in to her curiosity about the man.

He turned the mug around on the tabletop, speculatively. "Hard to say," he said finally.

"Ottawa winters might be a bit hard to take after five years in the Caribbean," she said, trying to draw him out.

"Hmm." He was refusing to be drawn. He was sipping his coffee as though he'd suddenly gotten all involved with it.

"Or maybe you like the cold," she persisted.

"Weather doesn't bother me much, one way or the other," he said. "I got used to cold in Helsinki, and heat in Cairo. Compared to them, Ottawa's climate is pretty tame."

Hilary raised her eyebrows. "What were you doing in Helsinki and Cairo?" she asked him. "More of 'this and that'?"

He flashed her a smile. "If I said I was working on some government contracts, would that satisfy you?" he said.

Most of Ottawa worked for the federal government, directly or indirectly, Hilary knew. It answered some of her questions, if not the most interesting ones. "It'll satisfy me temporarily, I guess," she said. "Especially since I have a feeling I'm not going to get any more out of you."

"Not on that subject, anyway."

"Quite the globe-trotter, aren't you?"

Something in his hazel eyes seemed suddenly torn and undecided. "You could call me that," he said. "I've covered most of the known world, in one way or another."

"I've hardly traveled at all," she confessed. And until just this moment, it hadn't really bothered her, she might have added. "Having two kids on your own really ties you down."

"Didn't your parents help out?"

Hilary looked at her own coffee mug, to avoid the piercing directness of his eyes. "In some ways," she said. "But they weren't happy with my getting married so young. They thought I should finish my education first, and they never liked Skip much. They took the boys for an occasional vacation, to give me a break, but basically they had a 'you made your bed, so lie in it' philosophy about the whole thing.''

''Are they still around?''

''No. My father died of a heart attack about six years ago, and my mother sort of faded after that. She was diagnosed with lung cancer just last year, and she went very quickly.'' She smiled. ''It's ironic. They would have disapproved strongly of my going out on a limb to start *Fortissimo,* but it was the little inheritance they left me that made me feel I could actually start the store at all.''

Mac was watching her closely, as if he wanted to read her mind and all the secrets in it. ''It must have hurt like hell, having them down on you like that,'' he said.

''I'm not asking for your sympathy, Mac.'' A trace of the irritation she'd felt with him earlier in the week surfaced again. ''I'm just saying that's why I haven't seen much of the world, that's all.''

''Would you like to? See the world, I mean?''

Mac felt a sudden eagerness jumping inside him. Maybe, after all, she wasn't as homebound as she made herself out to be.

She took her time considering the question. ''Part of me thinks it would be wonderful,'' she admitted finally. ''When you say Cairo, or the Caribbean, my mind conjures up all sorts of wonderful pictures, and that makes me want to take off and see some of those places for myself.'' She gave a self-deprecating laugh. ''I'm sure my mental images aren't anything like the real thing, of course.''

''Don't be so sure.'' He was leaning forward, elbows on the table on either side of his coffee mug. There was a new gleam in his eyes now. ''What do you think of when I say Cairo?''

She laughed again, getting caught up in the game. ''Dry, dusty heat,'' she said. ''Some musical instrument I can't identify wailing somewhere. Wonderful spicy food. Pretty romantic, right?''

"Also absolutely accurate."

"Oh, come on, Mac. I'm sure that's just what the tourist board wants you to think."

"It's more than that. Cairo *is* romantic. You should go there—one hot evening of wandering through those old streets and you'd be converted for life."

Mac's imagination had shot into top gear at the slight eager glow in her blue eyes. If he could convince her that life with a free-roving guy like himself had some appeal, maybe they weren't as far apart as he'd thought.

"And the Caribbean," he went on. "You can't believe the colors there, Hilary. Nothing in North America is remotely like it. Everything is brighter, more alive. And the sea is—well, there are almost as many colors of blue in it as there are in your eyes."

She was still laughing, and trying to sound firm. "My eyes are just plain blue," she argued.

"Plain blue!" He leaned a little closer, looking very deeply into them. "When I look into your eyes, I see the kind of light blue that you get in a Canadian sky on a hot, muggy summer day. And the brilliant blue you see from a sailboat in the waters between Ste. Helene and Martinique. And the indigo that beautiful women wear in—"

"Stop it, Mac." She held up a hand, smiling. "You're making this up."

He leaned a little farther, and grasped her hand. "I couldn't make up anything like what I see in your eyes," he said.

He saw her give a little gasp, and wished he could hold on to her hand longer. She reclaimed it, though, and wrapped both hands around her coffee mug.

"I'm beginning to think you must actually work for somebody's tourist board," she said, trying to sound cocky. "You certainly make a persuasive case for traveling."

"I haven't started to be persuasive yet," he said smoothly.

A hidden something was stirring inside Hilary now. God, she remembered that feeling from a hundred years ago—that sense that life was opening in front of her and all she had to do was step out into it.

She'd stepped into it, all right. Almost in the time it took to blink an eye, she'd become a single mother with two sons to support, and dreams had become more of a luxury than Mac could ever imagine.

"Out of everywhere you've been in the world, is there any one place you'd choose to go back to?" she asked him suddenly. She didn't want to frame the words *settle down,* but that was what she meant, and she could see that he knew it.

The word *Ottawa* wasn't exactly leaping to his lips, and that more or less told her what she'd wanted to know. "Ste. Helene was pretty appealing, before the coup," he said slowly. "Especially for someone who likes hot food."

"Do you think about going back there?"

He gave her a guarded smile. "To be honest, I don't think that far ahead," he said. "I kind of get blown all over the place, and make myself at home wherever I happen to end up."

At the moment, that happened to be at her kitchen table. Hilary was amazed at how natural it felt to be sitting here talking to him.

"And for the next year you're making yourself at home running a hot sauce store," she said. "What was the impulse behind that, Mac?"

The urge to tell her everything was almost physical in its strength. But he couldn't do it. The whole thing was just too delicate, too dicey. His chances for success depended on the whole world—including Hilary Gardiner—thinking he really was just a free spirit who'd happened to land in the retail trade.

"Hard to say," he hedged. "One thing's for sure, I had no idea there was even more paperwork involved in importing than there is in government work."

"Welcome to the real world." There was an edge to her voice now. "A minimal amount of research beforehand would have let you know what you were getting yourself into."

He wondered if he was going to have the nerve to show her the magazine article after all. He glanced around her small, neat kitchen, recognizing the hot sauce boxes that filled all the corners. This wasn't a home she could pick up and leave easily, or maybe ever. He was crazy even to think of Hilary Gardiner's future meshing with his.

He might as well get the bad news over with, then. Mac sighed, and said, "You're probably right. This whole business is completely new to me. And that's why I came to talk to you so early."

Hilary frowned. She'd almost forgotten to wonder why he *had* come, as if, even with all their differences, it was perfectly logical for Mac to be sitting and drinking her early-morning coffee with her at her kitchen table.

"What's going on?" she asked, not liking his suddenly serious tone.

He'd put a rolled-up magazine down on the table before sitting down, but she hadn't paid it much attention until now. "Do you get the Sunday magazine?" he asked, referring to a new publication that featured goings-on in Ottawa.

"Sure," she said. "They deliver it free to everybody, don't they?"

"I'm afraid so."

Mac's cryptic words made her increasingly nervous. She reached for the crumpled magazine, but he stopped her with a strong, tanned hand on her wrist.

"I guess yours hasn't gotten here yet," he said. "I was hoping I'd get here before it arrived."

"Mac, what are you talking about? Of all the mysterious game-playing—"

"It's not game-playing," he cut in. "It's pretty serious. Look, Hilary, I told them about your store. I really did. I insisted they interview you, too. But apparently they didn't bother."

Hilary's stomach fluttered a bit as she pulled her hand free and unrolled the magazine he'd brought.

"And I wanted to talk to you first, so you didn't get the idea I was trying to undercut you or anything."

She barely heard his words. She had an awful feeling she knew what she was going to see on the magazine's glossy cover.

"I guess it's just because I hit a trend, and that's what they went for." Mac's voice, in her ear, sounded eager, cajoling. "But I'm sure it's nothing more than a flash in the pan, Hilary. I just wanted you to know it wasn't my idea."

Mac's handsome face smiled up at her from the cover of the magazine that every household in Ottawa would be perusing with their coffee that Sunday morning. The photograph showed him standing in his shop, surrounded by Ste. Helenean specialties, looking every inch the successful small-business owner.

The caption was in a bold red that rivaled the robes of the expatriate islanders themselves. "The Hottest Shop In Town," it read, and underneath, in smaller letters, "MacDougall Scores a Coup."

Four

"Are you kidding me? He actually had the nerve to come and wave it under your nose?" There was sympathy and disbelief in Karen's tone.

"Well, he didn't exactly *wave* it. He said he wanted to break it to me gently, before I read it for myself."

"What a rat. Why didn't you tell me this before?"

Hilary sighed. It had been a couple of weeks since Mac had shown up on her doorstep that early Sunday morning, and she still wasn't sure about anything connected with his unexpected visit. Karen was the first person she'd even mentioned it to; the twins had stayed in their usual semi-comatose morning state until well after Mac had gone away again.

"I didn't think it was going to matter this much," she admitted. "A classic case of wishful thinking. I didn't want to believe one measly magazine article could make this much of a difference in our sales."

It was Saturday, and the two women had just finished closing up *Fortissimo* and going over the receipts for the week. Hilary would have been happier if the job had taken a little longer, but sales had been slim and getting slimmer for the past two weeks.

"What did you do when he showed you the article?" Karen asked, and immediately added, "And is he as good-looking as that picture made him seem?"

Hilary chose to answer her friend's first question and ignore the second. "I asked him to leave so I could think things over by myself," she said. "I didn't want him standing there watching me read the story."

"I can understand that. He must have been gloating like crazy."

"Actually he wasn't." Hilary didn't go into detail, but she couldn't forget the look in Mac's hazel eyes when he'd handed her the magazine with his picture on the cover. In the photograph he'd looked breezy and sure of himself, projecting that rakish charm that had been haunting her dreams. But in person he'd been honestly troubled. He'd known how the article was going to affect both *Fortissimo* and their relationship, such as it was. And he'd been bugged by it. It had made it very difficult to ask him to leave.

"So did he leave?" Karen was asking.

"Eventually."

Once again, Hilary slid over the detail of Mac's farewell kiss, because there was no way to describe the combination of longing and erotic fantasy she'd felt in that brief moment when his lips had touched hers. It had been a simple and undemanding caress, and yet ever since, she'd been thirsting for more.

"Well, the spy network tells me Mac's Hot Stuff has been doing a land-office business ever since that article appeared, so at least Mr. MacDougall has been too busy to bother you anymore," Karen said. The spies in question were Todd and Andrew, who'd volunteered for a couple of reconnaissance missions down to the Byward Market, to see what the competition was up to. Hilary hadn't been wild about the idea.

"I could have told you that without sending out the spies," she said ruefully to Karen now. "Mac really lucked into something at just the right moment. I'd give my left arm for a shipment of Ste. Helenean *poive* sauce at this point."

"No amputation, please. Things aren't that desperate yet." Karen looked over at the ledger Hilary had been updating. "Or are they?"

"Darned close. I didn't expect to break even in the first month, but there *are* bills to pay, and I was counting on a little cash coming in to pay them with." Something Karen had said was nagging at her, and she felt compelled to add, "You're wrong about one thing, though. I *have* heard from Mac since the day he brought the article by."

"You have?"

"Just on the phone. He keeps calling to see how we're doing."

"Of all the nerve—"

"And he's actually sent us a couple of customers. Remember the lady who wanted that barbecue sauce on Wednesday?"

"How could I forget? She was practically the only person who walked in the door on Wednesday, aside from the mailman."

"Well, anyway, Mac sent her over. I think it was a nice gesture."

Karen snorted. "One bottle of barbecue sauce at a $1.89 hardly makes up for all the people we lose because they head to Mac's place first and just stay there." Karen lowered her brows at her friend, apparently wondering why Hilary was bothering to defend a man they'd both agreed should be hung up in chains. "What gives, Hilary?" she asked. "*Is* the guy as good-looking as his picture?"

Once again Hilary sidestepped the question. Talking about it only made her ache inside at the thought of Mac's easy stance and laughing eyes. She closed the ledger, and said firmly, "If he is, it doesn't enter into anything at the moment. The point is, buddy, it's time to take some offensive action, or in six months' time there won't *be* any books for us to tally up on Saturday nights."

"What are you planning to do?"

Hilary took a deep breath. "I'm going to see if I can buy him out," she said.

The sentence sounded crazy to her own ears, and apparently to Karen's as well, from the *yawp* her friend gave. "You're going to *what?*"

"I can't think what else to do. I've got to head this off before it goes any further."

"Hilary, you said the other day you can't afford a new hose for your dishwasher. How are you going to buy out an entire store? And what makes you think the guy even wants to sell?"

"I'll take out a bank loan," Hilary said, fighting down the panicky feeling her own words called up in her. "And I think Mr. MacDougall will be open to negotiations. His heart isn't in this business. From what I can tell, the man hasn't settled in one place for a whole year since he got out of school. And he admitted himself that running a store is just a whim. I think I have a shot at it."

"Well, just make sure you're the one doing the shooting," Karen said. She sounded dubious. "If my impression of the handsome Mr. MacDougall is correct, he's a lot smarter than he's been letting on so far."

It wasn't too difficult to find him. Hilary connected a random phrase from the article about Mac's shop— "For now, MacDougall has settled on the top floor of a friend's house on Stanley Street"—with the street number she got by calling information. By eight-thirty the next morning she was on the front porch of a gray-stone house on Stanley Street, pressing the bell that said "MacDougall."

Mac was obviously a morning person. She remembered how chipper he'd been two weeks ago, when he'd invaded her kitchen before eight o'clock on a Sunday morning. In the back of her mind was the notion that it felt good to be turning the tables on him this way, marching unannounced into his world.

Of course, his world was a lot more upscale than hers. Hilary couldn't help thinking how big and solid all the houses on the street were. She knew the neighborhood; Stanley Street backed on the Rideau River, and the park there, with its old willows and winding paths, had been a favorite place for walking with her sons when they were smaller. She'd always liked the quiet dignity of the neighborhood. It was as if some prestige from the nearby Prime Minister's residence and Rideau Hall, the Governor General's mansion, rubbed off on the whole area.

She took in a deep breath now, trying not to feel like such a stranger in a part of town inhabited by diplomats and government insiders, when the oak door opened and she found herself looking at John Augustus Laurier Mac-Dougall dressed in nothing but a sheet.

He wasn't precisely dressed in it, but just clutching it around his waist. It left a great deal of him open to view—hard thigh muscles, broad, smooth shoulders, a hair-sprinkled torso that tapered tantalizingly to a pair of very lean hips, only one of which was actually covered by the off-white sheet. The other was bare, and as inviting to the touch as a sun-warmed curve of marble.

Hilary let her breath out all at once, without intending to. She was actually on the point of reaching out to him, and indulging in her sudden need to feel his hard, bare skin under her fingertips. Seeing him almost naked, with no warning, was doing crazy things to her thought processes.

For a moment she forgot who she was, or where she was. She let herself just gaze, completely immersed in her erotic and utterly uncharacteristic response to Mac's nearness. If someone had asked her what she was doing here, she'd have been hard-pressed to come up with an answer. *I'm lusting after the most beautiful male body I've ever seen,* might have been her unguarded reply.

Fortunately for Mac, he didn't ask that particular question. His first words were, "Oh, hell," and they didn't sound happy.

For the first time she took in the fact that while his body was in magnificent, pulse-warming condition, his face was the face of a man who had been deep in sleep two minutes ago. His curly hair was a mess, he was unshaven, and his eyes seemed to be having a hard time focusing on her. Hilary frowned.

"I'm sorry, Mac," she said. "I thought you were an early-morning type."

He leaned against the door frame and yawned mightily. "I guess you would," he said. His voice was thick with sleep.

She wanted to take a step back, but didn't. Leaning forward like that, he was too close for complete comfort. She could see the play of muscles in his forearm as he pushed it over his head and let it support him against the massive oak door frame. His other hand, pinning the sheet to his hip, kept drawing her attention. She was giddily aware of how great it would be if he lost his grip and let the sheet slide. She blinked, to clear the seductive vision from her mind.

Nervousness and arousal were making her chatty. "I'm sorry," she said again. "I remembered how wide-awake you were a couple of weeks ago, when you came to my place, and I wanted to talk to you, so I figured this would be a good time to catch you in, but if you'd rather I came back another time—"

The flood of words seemed to be too much for him. He stood up straight again and held up his left hand to slow her down.

"I'm not making this very clear, am I?" she said.

He shook his head, and made a noise in his throat that was somewhere between a groan and a growl. There was something primitive in the sound, something that didn't fit at all with this quiet, well-to-do street on a Sunday morning.

"Coffee first," Mac said, jerking his thumb in the direction of the broad staircase behind him. "Upstairs. Then talk."

In the time it took to climb two flights of stairs, Hilary found herself being swamped by more sexual fantasies than she'd had in her life up to this moment. Following behind Mac made it impossible not to watch the shifting of his muscles, or to notice the fact that his golden tan covered every inch of him that she could see. Since there were very few inches of him she *couldn't* see, that made it tempting to imagine him sprawled naked on a white-sand beach somewhere, bathing in the warm tropical sunshine.

By the time they reached an open door on the top floor she was breathing hard, and picturing herself stretched out on that beach beside him, feeling the sun and Mac's eyes warming some formerly very secret parts of her body.

The hell of it was, she thought, the man wasn't even trying to be sexy. He was clearly only half-conscious, padding up the stairs like a bear who hasn't realized yet that spring has sprung. But somehow his every move, from the drive of his lean hips to the welcoming gesture he made—open palm ushering her in the door—had the power to turn careful, goal-oriented Hilary into a wild woman who was at the mercy of her own inner imaginings.

"Coffee," he said again, sounding marginally more awake. "Filters. Beans."

His gesture shifted to the kitchen area of the big open apartment. Hilary could see the coffee apparatus on the counter.

"You want me to make it?" she asked.

"Please."

Obviously his being so wide-awake two Sundays ago had been a fluke. Hilary contrasted his nearly monosyllabic utterances this morning with his usual talkative ways, and smiled to herself. She moved into the kitchen, and tried not to notice how close he was to stepping on the trailing edge of the sheet as he walked over to the mattress on the floor and picked up his blue jeans and a shirt. One false step and the sheet would be history, she thought wickedly, and marveled at the secret pleasure she was getting out of the idea.

He managed to keep his grip as he headed across the big main room and through a door. A moment later Hilary heard the sound of running water, and surmised that he was counting on a shower to wake him up. She found the coffeepot, filters, grinder and beans, and by the time he returned, dressed in his jeans and a light khaki shirt, she had coffee ready for both of them.

His fingers brushed hers as he took the steaming mug from her hands. She'd been expecting the touch of warm skin that she remembered so achingly, and she was astonished to feel that his fingertips were icy cold, on this warm July morning.

Her eyes widened. Had he been taking a *cold* shower? Her own hidden erotic fantasies were all very well, but the idea that Mac had been entertaining the same realization was very unsettling. She watched him as he took a sip of his coffee, fascinated by the way he moved. He had a trick of making his gestures bold and economical all at the same time, she thought. His dark brown hair, almost black now from the shower, swept back from his forehead and gave his face a new and almost boyish look.

Hilary cleared her throat. "I should have called first," she said. "I didn't realize—"

"Hold it." He made a wait-a-minute gesture again, and took a deeper sip of coffee. Then he took in and let out a deep breath, and smiled at her. "There we go," he said. "Awake at last. You make good coffee, lady."

"Thank you, sir." She took a sip of her own coffee, completely unaware of whether it was good or undrinkable. His smile was making those butterflies start to cavort around inside her again.

"You're right," he said. "Usually I *am* awake in the mornings. But usually I don't stay up most of the night partying, or not anymore, anyway."

That explained the bleary look in his eyes when he'd first opened the door, she thought. She glanced around the open top-floor apartment, with its kitchen nook and the double-size mattress plunked down in solitary splendor in front of the bank of windows that faced the backyard. There was virtually no other furniture, no pictures, no books, almost no other signs that anyone lived here. A few items of clothing, a card table, a couple of chairs, and minimal kitchen equipment, of which the coffee-making tools were by far the most extensive.

"Partying here?" she couldn't help asking. This was such a strangely empty place for such a sociable man to have landed himself in.

He shook his head. "We started at Domingo's," he said. "Some friends of friends had just arrived from the islands. They'd gotten off Ste. Helene when the coup happened, but it took them some time to drum up the airfare to get to Canada. They wanted to celebrate."

He scrunched up his features, then shook his head as if trying to clear out the effects of the celebrating.

"You can say what you like about the pace of life down there," he said, "but there is one thing everybody admits. Folks from Ste. Helene really do know how to party." She couldn't tell, from his tone, whether he was admiring that trait or regretting it. "I didn't get home until after four."

And she'd been ringing his doorbell at eight-thirty. Hilary put a hand over his, making the spontaneous touch before she'd had time to think about it. "Next time I'll call first," she said. "I promise."

He looked up, seeming startled. Now that he was fully awake, his eyes were starting to take on that humorous, perceptive twinkle that had put her on her guard the first time she'd met him. The hazel light in them made her wish she hadn't touched him quite so readily. By the time she decided to withdraw her hand, though, it was too late. He'd closed his own fingers around it, and she was caught.

"Does that mean you think there will be a next time?" he quizzed her.

Hilary had to think hard to remember anything at all about why she'd come here in the first place. "Yes," she said, breathily. "At least, if you agree to what I'm proposing. I think we might have more reasons to get together."

Damn it, this was coming out all wrong. She'd intended to be businesslike and practical in laying down her idea about buying out Mac's Hot Stuff. Instead, not only did her voice sound like she'd just run a marathon, but she was phrasing her suggestion as though it had something to do with bed instead of business.

She tried to get hold of her thoughts, and to tell herself it didn't matter that Mac's bed was only ten feet from where they sat. The fact that he'd been sleeping in it twenty minutes ago, and that the mattress was probably still warm and holding the musky scent of his skin didn't mean a thing in the context of this discussion.

Mac couldn't figure Hilary out this morning. He'd gotten himself more or less under control now. It was one thing to be wakened by the doorbell in the middle of a dizzily erotic dream about a woman with dark hair and blue eyes. It was another to find that woman standing on your doorstep looking at you with a combination of innocence and allure that was enough to tempt a stronger man than Mac.

A cold shower had temporarily taken care of the problem of his physical reaction to her presence. But it couldn't explain all the things he was feeling inside, or why he was so reluctant to let go of her hand now that he had it.

"What exactly are you proposing?" he asked.

Hilary cleared her throat again. "I want to buy out your store," she said bluntly.

Mac stared at her. Then he laughed. "This is a joke, right?" he said. "To test whether I'm still asleep?"

"I'm serious, Mac." She managed to get her hand back, and wrapped it tensely around her mug. "I've done the calculations. I think I can just about swing it, if I'm careful."

"And lucky."

She looked up at him with suddenly angry eyes. "Luck is what I'm planning to buy," she said. "Your luck, to be specific."

He sighed. "Hilary, I'm lucky because I have connections on Ste. Helene. I can't sell you those."

It took a few minutes of wrangling to convince her that he wasn't going to listen to any offers to buy his store. By that time, the disappointment he could see in her dark blue eyes was tearing him apart inside.

"But *why?*" she kept asking him. "It's obviously not what you want to do with your life. You're not even planning to continue it after this year is up."

He admitted that. "It's not negotiable," he told her. "You'll just have to believe me on that point."

Her face set in a stubborn look that would have been almost girlish if it hadn't been for the sensuous fullness of her lower lip. "How about this, then?" she said. "If we're going to split the market, let's split it fair and square. You sell me some of your Ste. Helenean stuff, and start branching out into other sauces yourself. That way we'll be competing on an even basis."

He considered the idea. From her point of view, he supposed it made perfect sense. Unfortunately she didn't know the whole story, and he couldn't tell her how important it was that he keep up a front of being an exclusive dealer in Ste. Helenean foods. Besides, if word got out that she was stocking the Ste. Helenean community, she'd be a target for the same kinds of surveillance he knew he'd been under lately. He couldn't possibly let her take that risk, even unknowingly.

"I'm sorry," he said. "I'm just not interested in branching out. And things are so tight with the export folk on Ste. Helene that it's all I can do to get enough stock for the customers I've got. I'm sorry, Hilary."

Apologies were clearly not cutting any ice with her, and he couldn't say he was surprised.

"I knew there was a possibility you'd say this," she said. There was a coldness in her voice that made him cringe. "But somehow I had hoped you'd be willing to compromise a little. It's clear you don't have to make any money out of that store of yours. Nobody goes into business for just one year if they're really trying to turn a profit. So why not give me a break, instead of trying to run me into the ground? This means an awful lot to me, Mac."

Her voice quavered a little on the last sentence, and Mac couldn't help reaching for her hand again, as if his touch could reassure her even though his words could not.

"If I could see any way to help out, I'd do it," he said. He was being perfectly honest, even though he couldn't tell her the real reason for his refusal to help. "But I just can't. Hang in there, Hilary, and I'm sure your store will make a go of it."

"Damn you!" She set her mug down on the countertop so hard that Mac wouldn't have been surprised to see shards of glass flying from it. The Caribbean softness was gone from her eyes now; they were the color of blue ice.

"I can understand you wanting to protect your own interests," she said. "But I'd rather you didn't bother apologizing to me about it. If you're really concerned about me, Mac, there are several things you could do to help. And if you're not willing to do them, then please don't pretend you're concerned."

She'd reclaimed her hand again, and was draining her coffee mug with the air of a woman taking a last drag on her cigarette before execution. Mac found himself more torn than he'd been in fifteen years of work for the External Affairs Department. He'd never been faced with a conflict between his job and his emotions before now, and the strain of it was almost enough to make him tell her the whole story right then and there.

Almost. A lifetime of training and example wasn't something he could shrug off in an instant. But it was just as impossible to let Hilary go without trying to make her understand how he felt about her.

"Hilary, wait."

She'd started to head for the door, chin high, handbag swinging angrily at her hip. Her throat was creamy and smooth at the open collar of her off-white blouse. He could see the agitation of her pounding pulse there. Her waist, where the blouse tucked into her freshly pressed jeans, was tiny and inviting. He caught up with her, spanned her waist with his two hands, and turned her to face him.

She was startled, and still upset. "What do you think you're doing?" she demanded.

"Changing your mind."

"Good luck."

Mac couldn't help smiling. She felt so damn *right*, held close to him like this. And she'd just fed him a line he had a ready answer for. "As I've already pointed out, I'm a lucky guy," he said. He saw her eyes widen, and before she could answer, he pulled her even closer. His arms slid naturally around her. Her hair smelled so sweet, like wild violets in spring.

Mac's pulse was racing again, the way it had been when she'd wakened him. He felt himself sliding back into the dream world where he'd been making love with Hilary, drowning in pleasures he hadn't known could be so draining and so satisfying all at once. Dream spilled over into reality when he brushed a hand over her satiny dark hair and felt the softness of her skin under his fingertips.

"God, you're beautiful," he said roughly. There was wonder in his tone. "Don't run away, Hilary. Not just yet."

He saw her eyes half close. Somehow that only intensified their blueness. He felt her battling the passions inside her, as she must have battled them through long years of struggling with life on her own. *You're going to lose the fight this time, sweetheart,* he wanted to say. She couldn't fight against her own desires and his, too, and she seemed to know it.

The thought made him feel exultant, kingly. He lowered his lips to hers with a heady certainty that she'd welcome his kiss.

And she did. Her lips parted, invited him to probe further, to make her moan with unsatisfied need. He heard the hunger in the soft sounds she was making, and his whole body roared into a response that he couldn't have denied if he'd wanted to. He was crushing her against him now, exploring her curves with an urgent touch, as though he still couldn't quite believe she was real. Every kiss, every gasp she gave, plunged him farther back into his dream, farther away from any attempt at remembering reality.

She was going with him every step of the way. He felt her fingers in his hair, warm against its dampness. She lifted her chin, and he kissed the creamy stretch of her neck, letting the touch of his tongue excite them both as he found the spot where her pulse hammered wildly against her skin.

Nothing had ever pushed him to such an agony of arousal as the way her slender body moved against him. He wanted more, he wanted all of her. Holding her fast, he flicked open the buttons of her blouse and let his mouth explore the cool softness of her skin. His hand brushed over her breasts, and returned to savor the tight knots of desire that he could feel in their centers.

The silky blouse was suddenly an obstacle that had to be gotten rid of. He tugged it free of her waistband, and heard her moan as his hands slid over her rib cage, over the lace of her bra. Only two more buttons stood between him and that unimaginably smooth expanse of skin.

His mind was racing like an overheated engine. He had to get rid of his own shirt, too, and know the exquisite pleasure of feeling his bare torso against hers. Could the sensation possibly rival the mindless eroticism of his dreams? He was sure it would.

His hand was grappling with those last two stubborn buttons when he became aware that Hilary was trying to slow him down. "Mac, wait," she said.

Waiting was something Mac was lousy at. His actions confirmed that now, and he kept at the buttons until she leaned back in his grasp and closed her small fingers over his, stopping his movements.

"I mean *wait,*" she said. There was quiet authority in her voice, oddly contrasting with the breathless quaver of unsatisfied desire. The combination finally stopped him, and he lifted his head and looked at her.

Her eyes were dark with passion, wide with confusion. He couldn't tell whose heartbeat he was feeling against his ribs, hers or his own. All he knew was that he wanted this woman, wanted everything about her with a wildness that almost scared him.

"What do you mean, wait?" he demanded. Something was lodged in his throat, and it made his words come out more harshly than he'd intended.

"I mean, this is just going too fast." She let out a long breath, and wrapped her arms around his neck again. He answered the gesture naturally, sliding his arms around her and pulling her close. His imagination still reeled with the scent and softness of her. It made it very difficult to concentrate on what she was saying.

"I don't think either one of us has thought this through," she said. Her voice was low and as husky as his own. "Part of me is saying 'To hell with thinking about it at all, and let's just make love if we want to.'"

He gave a growl and buried his face in her neck, hoping she would understand that he was voting for the part of her that was saying "let's make love if we want to."

She understood it, all right. He heard her say, "Oh, God," and felt her tilt her head to one side, reveling in his caress. Apparently, though, even her admitted pleasure wasn't going to get in the way of her habitual common sense.

"This is crazy, Mac," she gasped. "We have to stop."

He stopped moving suddenly, lips still grazing the base of her neck. "I've stopped," he said thickly.

"You rat." She gave a shaky laugh, and shook her head. "You're making this very difficult."

"I thought I was making it simpler."

"Look at me, Mac."

With an effort, he lifted his head. This time her eyes were serious, and damnably under control.

"You think you want me, but do you really?"

He nodded vigorously, and she laughed again.

"Be serious," she told him.

"I am serious. I want you, and you want me. See? It's simple, like I told you."

"Do you want everything about me? Do you want my mortgage payments and my two teenage sons and my twelve-hour days at the shop?"

"It wasn't your mortgage payments I was lusting after, lady."

"You know what I mean, and don't pretend you don't."

She was right. Mac let his grip loosen marginally, despite the desire that was still zinging through him.

"And part of me wants you, very much. But I don't want the way you run your life, Mac. I don't want anything to do with picking up and taking off halfway around the world. So you see—" The breath she drew in was unsteady. "It just wouldn't work."

Damn the woman, she was making far too much sense. And none of it applied to the things he felt when he held her close, or explained why the usually worldly-wise John Augustus Laurier MacDougall was willing to fling aside every bit of savvy and experience he had just for the chance to hold Hilary Gardiner in his arms.

"You seem pretty sure about that," he said gruffly.

"Can you deny that I'm right?"

He only grunted in reply, and finally let her free. She moved away from him as though a gate had been held open for a limited time only and she knew she had to get through it.

"I'm sorry, Mac," she said gently. "I guess we're right back where we started, aren't we?"

He shook his head. "No, ma'am, we're not," he told her. "And neither one of us can pretend we are. Not after what just happened."

"What just happened was—very nice."

Mac almost laughed. "That's like saying a tropical rainstorm can be very damp," he said.

"You know what I meant. 'Nice' was the best I could do on the spur of the moment. But it isn't going to happen again. It can't."

"No?" He cocked an eyebrow at her, challenging her.

"No. In fact, I don't see that there's much reason for us to see each other any more. It might be better if we don't."

He had an answer already up his sleeve for that one. "What about Saturday night?" he said.

"Saturday night?" She looked blank.

"The Chamber of Commerce reception for new Ottawa businesses. I assume you're going to be there."

"I'd forgotten all about it." There was dismay on her face now, as if she'd honestly convinced herself it was better for them not to see each other again, and now she was faced with the idea that she couldn't end things quite so neatly and abruptly.

"Well, I hadn't. And I expect to see you there, so don't try coming up with any reasons why you can't go."

She had rebuttoned her blouse and had moved toward the door. As she placed a hand on the doorknob, her other hand gripped the strap of her handbag, and he could see that the knuckles were white. "You're a very unsettling man, Mr. MacDougall," she told him.

He couldn't help grinning. "Always have been," he said. "Always will be, too."

From the look on her face, as she said goodbye, that was one promise she'd be just as happy for him not to keep.

Five

Not since she'd bought her first bikini at seventeen had Hilary felt so naked in a public place. She turned slowly in front of the department-store mirrors, and watched the low-cut green dress swirl and drape itself around her. She barely trusted the thin straps to keep the dark crepe sheath on her body.

"I don't know, guys," she said. "Cost aside, don't you think there's something a little funny about two teenage boys dragging their mother out to buy clothes?"

"There'll be a lot of fancy people at this reception," Todd pointed out. "It's a good chance to score points for *Fortissimo*."

"And anyway, if you don't buy this, what will you wear?" Andrew added practically. "That plain old blue suit, right?"

Hilary had been about to say "My blue suit." The blue suit was serviceable, durable, and well-cut. She'd bought it about eight years ago, to wear to the office at the university. She tried to picture herself in it now, and failed. All she could see was the beguiling drape of the green crepe dress, and the way the loose folds of the neckline seemed to make her skin look softer and her waistline smaller at the same time. The blue suit belonged on some other planet.

"It's on sale, Mom," Andrew pointed out.

"Right. Now it only costs half a mortgage payment, instead of most of one."

"Think of it as a business expense."

"Think of what Mac will say about it," Todd added.

Hilary turned an eagle eye on the two of them. "I'm not spending money on a dress just to impress Mac," she said sternly.

"Hey, whatever." Todd backed away quickly, warned by the look in his mother's eye. "It's just that when we went down there to scout out his place, he seemed awful interested in how you were doing. That's all."

Hilary debated whether the subject was worth pursuing. She decided it wasn't. She had to admit, in all honesty, that Todd and Andrew could be just as deviously charming as Mac himself, when they put their minds to it.

Worse yet, she had to admit to herself that Todd was right. She *was* thinking about how the emerald-green crepe dress would look to Mac's eyes. She turned once more in front of the mirrors, and smiled. "All right," she said. "Let's dust off the plastic money, and take this baby home."

At night, the new National Gallery looked like a postmodern castle. Hilary had been trying to make time to get to the gallery ever since it had opened, but tonight was the first time she'd actually set foot in the long stone-and-glass structure, with its multileveled glass pagoda rising at one end.

The Chamber of Commerce reception was in the big open rotunda, under the huge glass turrets. Enormous purple and red banners hung from the peak of the roof, softening the gray stone and giving the place the air of a dignified carnival.

As Hilary headed up the long ramp to the rotunda, she could hear the relaxed beat of music over the clicking of her own high heels on the stone floor. There was a crowd already mingling in the large open space, and between the formal blacks and whites of tuxedos and the gentle glow of women's gowns, she could see a steel band dressed in ebullient red. *I know that color,* she thought. She couldn't help connecting the vibrant Ste. Helenean red with Mac.

The receptionist fastened a name tag to Hilary's slinky green dress, and introduced her to some of the Chamber of Commerce officials who were greeting the business owners. "Hot sauce, eh?" one of them said cordially. "I think I've been by your place. It's down in the market, isn't it?"

"Actually, I'm up on Wellington." It took an effort to keep a polite smile on her face. Was this whole evening going to be just more proof of how likely it was that Mac's store was going to drive her out of business?

"Oh, I'm thinking of someone else. Young MacDougall, isn't it?"

Hilary nodded and steered the conversation toward other things.

"Young MacDougall" was nowhere to be seen. Hilary found herself chatting with elected officials, bureaucrats, and a surprising number of local and national celebrities. She also encountered a couple of friends from her days at the University of Ottawa.

"Whew!" she sighed, as she and a former classmate rested their feet by sitting down at a small table on the sidelines. "I'm glad I dressed up. I had no idea there would be so many big names here."

"They're trying to prove the grass-roots economy's as strong as ever," her friend said. "That's why they drummed up the names. I gather old Senator MacDougall made the opening remarks, but I didn't get here early enough to catch them."

Hilary sat up straighter. She remembered that Mac's impressive list of names had sounded vaguely familiar to her when he'd first introduced himself, and now she realized why.

"Augustus Laurier MacDougall," she said, half under her breath.

"Right." Her friend looked puzzled. "You remember, he used to be Finance Minister a hundred years ago. And then he was a diplomat, an ambassador, I think, and now he's in the Senate. His son's around here somewhere, too. I saw him chatting up one of the P.M.'s top aides." A cloud passed across her face. "Oops, did I put my foot in it? I forgot you guys are supposed to be competitors or something."

"Or something," Hilary agreed vaguely. "Excuse me, okay, Cynthia? I have to go see a man about a mystery."

Her friend waved goodbye, but Hilary barely saw it. There had been a lot of questions about Mac that she hadn't really looked into very deeply, and now she was beginning to see the answers to some of them. How had a man with no job and apparently no roots managed to come up with a big enough stake to start a store in a very expensive part of town? Why had he settled in the area of Ottawa near the embassies, the official residences, the diplomats' homes? What was behind his globe-trotting all these years?

His connection to a well-known Canadian politician and diplomat might explain a lot of that. It also raised some new and even more troubling questions. It made her wonder exactly what Mac was doing back in Ottawa in the first place. The episode of the motorcycle chase three weeks ago pushed its way back into her mind.

It took her a while to find him, because the crowd had thickened and there was a lot of intense social mingling going on. A few couples were dancing to the easy beat of the steel band's music, and there was a growing crush in front of the buffet tables. Hilary moved through the crowd until her watchful gaze snagged on a pair of shoulders she would have recognized anywhere.

Tonight they were clad in an extremely well-tailored tux jacket, which didn't quite manage to disguise the sexy stance she knew was underneath. His hair was neatly combed, but there was still the hint of a sea breeze about him, somehow. Hilary pushed through the throng, and came up beside him just in time to hear him deliver a long and apparently passionately felt statement in flawless French.

That caught her off guard. Her own French was minimal, but she knew enough to realize that Mac's Québecois accent was good enough to be classed as perfect. The man he was talking to was nodding seriously, and replying animatedly. Hilary was sure she'd seen his face on the news recently, although she couldn't quite place it.

It was obvious that he and Mac were deeply engrossed in their conversation. Hilary started to move away again, but before she could leave, and without even glancing her way, Mac shot out a hand and gripped her wrist.

"Don't go," he said. "I've been looking for you."

He kept hold of her as he performed introductions, switching between French and English with practised ease. Hilary found herself shaking hands with the well-known former politician who'd just finished heading up a special commission on the state of small business in Canada.

"Mac flatters me by speaking in French," he said to Hilary in thickly accented English. "But my English will do, yes?"

"It's better than my French," Hilary confessed.

The conversation picked up where it had left off, and ranged over issues that Hilary would have sworn Mac knew nothing about: international economics, tariffs, interprovincial relations. She was looking at him with a growing astonishment by the time the other man shook her hand again and moved on. Not only was Mac's manner smooth, polished, and engagingly diplomatic, but he seemed to know exactly what he was talking about. The man never ceased to surprise her.

"And here I thought you didn't give a hoot about the business world," she said, when they were alone.

He shrugged, looking a little embarrassed. "I read the newspaper," he said. "You pick up stuff that way."

"I read the paper, too," she told him, "but that doesn't mean I have the inside track on things. And it sounds to me as if you do."

He waved away the pointed comment. "I get carried away," he said. "I start spouting opinions as though I really knew what I was talking about. I didn't realize I was getting away with it quite so well."

That was baloney, but she didn't say so. She was getting distracted by the closeness of him, and the way he was looking at her. She recalled the strength of his fingers as he'd encircled her wrist a few minutes ago. Her skin seemed to tingle there with the mere memory of it.

She was surprised to find her heart beating a little faster, as though they were sharing something intimate even in the midst of the people all around them. Or maybe it was *because* of the crowd that their private exchange seemed so special.

He leaned a little closer as he added, "And I didn't realize you had a fairy godmother, either."

"If you mean the dress, I don't. I have a credit card and two sons who refused to let me show up here tonight in an old blue linen suit."

"You have more than that, Hilary. You have the magic to carry off something as provocative as that dress and still look as innocent as a rose. Just looking at you has me jumping out of my skin, and if there weren't so damn many people around, I'd take you in my arms and prove it to you right now."

By the time he'd finished, Hilary's knees were weak. There was something inside her, something she'd kept tightly guarded and firmly in hand for a long time, that seemed to dissolve on contact whenever Mac leveled those hazel eyes at her.

And then, having reduced her to a speechless state of longing and lust, he said casually, "I'm starving. Want to join me in some supper?"

She followed him into the pack around the food table, and finally found her tongue again. "I might have known I'd find you near the food," she said.

"Not just food." He shot her that devil-may-care grin over his shoulder, and finished off what was left of her equilibrium. "*Hot* food."

Not just any hot food, she discovered a moment later. Once they'd squeezed their way to the table, Hilary could see pieces of meat on little skewers and deep-fried plantain rings. It all looked familiar, especially the array of sauce bottles ringing the table. Ste. Helene strikes again, she thought. Somehow her appetite was suddenly less keen.

Mac's wasn't. He was piling a plate high with everything in sight, and joking with the man serving behind the table. When the man switched into a characteristic, deeply accented French that Hilary recognized as Ste. Helenean, Mac followed right along.

She turned away, wanting to sort out her thoughts on her own. It was one thing to think of Mac as a handsome pirate who'd sailed the seven seas and wherever else there was to sail. It was quite different to discover that he might be a member of the Ottawa establishment, connected somehow to the diplomatic world. She'd been half in love with the romantic image she'd conjured up for him, and now she was getting closer to the reality of who and what he really was. Her head hurt suddenly, with the pressure of all her unanswered questions.

Her vision swam with red for a moment, and she blinked to clear it. Mac's friend Sarah was standing in front of her, a welcoming but uncertain smile on her face and her usual bright red costume on.

"Hello, Hilary," she said gravely. "You don't want to try any skewered goat tonight?"

"Oh, thank you, Sarah." Hilary tried to get herself under control. "Maybe I'll just nibble on Mac's. It looks like he's taken enough for a small army."

Sarah's even white teeth showed as her smile widened. "That Mac, he loves to eat. It's a pleasure to cook for him."

For the first time Hilary wondered just what Mac and Sarah's friendship was all about. She didn't think it was romantic, but there was definitely something about it that she didn't understand.

"I guess Ste. Helenean cooking is trendy enough now that the Chamber of Commerce decided to jump on the bandwagon, too," she said casually. "It all looks great, Sarah."

"Thank you, Hilary. Having us cater here was Mac's idea, actually. He knows everybody in Ottawa, that one."

She tossed an indulgent smile in Mac's direction, and moved on to encourage a reluctant-looking Chamber of Commerce official to try the fried plantains.

Hilary waited until Mac had disengaged himself from the throng and then followed him to a quiet table. She watched him eat, absently noting just how much hot sauce he was pouring on his skewered meat from the small bottle he'd brought along from the buffet table. She was so quiet that Mac finally asked her what was on her mind.

"I was just thinking that for someone who claims to be such a novice at retailing, you have a pretty good instinct for self-promotion," she said. "Or maybe if you have enough contacts, you don't have to work very hard to get free advertising."

He finished the bite he was eating, swallowed, and looked hard at her. "You're talking about my getting Sarah to cater the reception, aren't you?"

"You know I am."

He spread his hands. "It's promotion for Sarah and Domingo's, not for me," he said. "They're new in Ottawa, and it's tough to make money in the restaurant business. I thought this would give them a boost."

"And of course, since you're the only supplier of Ste. Helenean food in the city, it'll give you a boost, too," she pointed out.

"That wasn't my plan."

"Let me say it again—for someone without a plan, you're doing pretty darned well."

She couldn't keep the edge out of her voice. She tried to look around her, at the huge glass tower above them, at the animated faces of the guests, at the red banners that hung from the rafters. But all she could see was Mac's open hazel gaze, and the restless way he was tapping his fork on the edge of his plate.

"Try a plantain," he said finally.

"I'm not all that hungry."

"They're great, really."

"I believe you. But I ate before I came."

"Just one."

She wanted to smile at his wheedling tone, but she refused to give in. He was trying to evade the subject she'd raised, and she didn't want to let him get away with it. If he was this slippery now, how was she ever going to find out what the rest of his life was really all about?

"You're right." He changed his tack. "I put an awful lot of hot sauce on these. They're probably too hot for you."

"I know what you're doing, Mac."

"No, seriously. Remember, the other night, I liked stuff a little hotter than you did. This is probably past your threshold."

"This is a cheap trick, MacDougall."

"Hey, I don't mind. I wouldn't want you to eat anything that might burn your—"

She rolled her eyes at him, then reached for one of his fried plantains and popped it into her mouth. Her years of training stood her in good stead. The biting sauce made her vision blur momentarily, but she managed to swallow it without disgracing herself by yelping or begging for a glass of water.

"Really," Mac was going on, as if she hadn't moved. "We all have our limits, and I think it's good that you know yours."

"Stop it." She hit him playfully on the arm, and gave in to the smile he'd been trying to coax out of her. "Next you're going to be saying 'Here comes the little airplane' and trying to get me to open my mouth by pretending to be the hangar. I know all the tricks, Mac. Remember, I've fed two boys for a lot of years now."

"I don't believe it." He was grinning back, pleased with himself. "It's not possible for you to be the mother of those two strapping hunks. You clearly just hired them to throw me off the track."

"Darn," she said. "And I thought I was being so clever."

"You're dealing with a trained professional, honey." Before Hilary could ask him just what, exactly, he was a trained professional *at*, he went on, "And since you're clearly really only sixteen years old, I'm hoping you're too young and innocent to see through my next ploy. Because I'm going to ask you to step up to my apartment with me, if you don't have any objections."

Her heart rate started its quick climb again. "And have some Madeira, m'dear?" she asked him, still smiling. She felt suddenly frivolous, irresponsible, as impractical and beautiful as her new green dress. And she knew it was all because of the smile in Mac's eyes.

"Something like that," he said. There was hope in his face, too, and just the merest trace of uncertainty. Hilary found herself wanting crazily to indulge the hope, and erase the uncertainty. She told herself sternly that leaving the party and going to Mac's would be a good opportunity to pry some answers out of her mysterious buccaneer. But in her bones and her blood, she knew the simple truth. She just wanted to be alone with him.

"All right," she said, and felt her pulse quicken a little more. "Give me one more of those fried plantains, and let's go. And put some more sauce on this one, all right? That last one was a bit tame."

Six

——

Her frivolous mood had evaporated somewhat by the time they got to Mac's. They drove there in Hilary's car, and there was a sudden awkwardness between them as they settled down next to each other in the small vehicle, as though neither of them was quite sure where they were headed next.

"Along St. Patrick's your best bet," Mac said, pointing.

"I know." Hilary turned the wheel. "No motorcycle tonight, Mac?"

He looked down at his immaculate outfit. "Doesn't go with the tux," he said briefly. "I took a cab."

They were silent for the rest of the ride.

There were no lights on in Mac's house when they arrived, upstairs or down. "You have pretty quiet landlords," Hilary commented. She remembered the silence of the lower floors from her earlier visit here.

Mac turned his key in the lock, and opened the door. "Actually they're not around these days," he said. "They got posted to Mexico City, just about the time I came back to Ottawa. They offered me their house while they're away."

"Posted? You mean, as diplomats."

"Yeah." He didn't seem to want to elaborate. "Anyway, they told me to go ahead and use the whole house, but I just couldn't get used to spreading out and having actual furniture and stuff. I guess I've been living out of a suitcase for too long. So I just took over the top floor, since it was empty, and made myself at home up there."

Knowing they were alone in this big old house gave an extra edge to the thought of spending the evening with Mac. Hilary followed him up the two flights of stairs and into his open top-floor apartment.

Mac liked coming back into this big room at night. He paused, as he often did, before turning on the lights.

"I hope you don't mind the dark for a minute," he said. "I get a kick out of this view at night."

He watched Hilary step forward to the three big French windows that overlooked the river. In the near-darkness she moved like something out of a dream, with her green dress floating around her.

"I can understand why," she said. "This is beautiful, Mac. I didn't realize you could see the Parliament Buildings from up here. And I've always loved those old willows down by the river. They're so big, and so permanent looking."

He gave a short laugh, and joined her by the windows. "I've always *dis*liked them, for precisely that reason," he said. "Who wants things that have been rooted to the same spot for a hundred years?"

"Some people find that appealing," she said softly.

"Well, I'm not one of them." It seemed important to make that clear to her. In spite of everything he was feeling—the way his head spun slightly when she turned to look at him with those luminous blue eyes, the way his loins tightened at the thought of holding her close to him and feeling the curves and hollows of her through the draping of her dress—in spite of all that, he knew their worlds were still an ocean apart. He couldn't lie to her about that.

She watched him silently for a long moment, and then turned back to the night view. "The Peace Tower lights look so pretty reflecting on the river," she said. "And I've always thought the External Affairs building was sort of grim, like a big battleship, but in this light it's actually almost romantic."

He couldn't help smiling at that. "Romantic is about the last word I'd use to describe External," he said.

From the sharp way she turned to face him, he realized she'd chosen her words carefully, and he'd played right into her hands. "And how *does* a fly-by-night traveler like you describe External Affairs?" she said pointedly. "Or do you just get your impressions of it from the newspapers, along with what you know about international economics?"

Damn it, he hadn't wanted to lie to her, but that didn't mean he wanted to tell her the whole truth, either. Deep down, he was afraid that if she knew everything about him, she'd pick up the handbag and shawl she'd dropped casually on his counter, and walk out the door. And he couldn't stand the thought of that. Just being here alone with her, close together in the soft light of a summer night, was sweeter than anything Mac could remember. He didn't want it to end, not yet.

"Maybe I just got my impressions of External Affairs from looking out the window at their building," he said carefully. And then, before she could come up with another question he didn't want to answer, he moved nearer to her.

At first he only meant to drink in the honeyed perfume of her hair. She wore it loose tonight, and it hung to her bare shoulders like a glossy banner. Mac's eyes closed as he took in the scent of it, and he felt that jolt of pleasure again.

He moved closer. His hands grazed her shoulders, felt her shiver slightly, tightened their hold and pulled her against him.

"Cold?" he asked softly.

"No." The word came out on a sigh. "Why do I get the feeling you're changing the subject, Mac?"

"Because I was bored with it. I thought we'd move on to something more interesting."

He lowered his head. His lips found the silk of her skin, caressed the base of her neck, hungered for more. He opened his eyes halfway and his gaze rested on the loose folds of her neckline. Somehow this damn dress managed to be decorous even while it revealed practically everything about Hilary's graceful figure. From his vantage point he could see the swell of her breasts, and it was driving him wild.

"Mac, wait—"

Impossible. He'd been thinking of doing this ever since she appeared by his side in the crowd at the reception, and now that he was tasting the sweetness of her skin, and hearing the deep breaths that caught at her throat, he knew he couldn't stop.

"Hilary," he said, and her name was a caress in itself. He ran his hand along the length of her arm, and felt her fingers tighten eagerly around his when he reached her hand. "Hilary, don't tell me you don't want this. If you try—" He spoke against her ear, and felt her shudder deeply. "If you try, I won't believe you."

His free hand smoothed back her hair, glanced over her shoulder, moved lower, and found the intoxicating roundness of her breasts. His gasp of pleasure mingled with hers then, and he felt the tide of longing inside him turn to a raging flood, pounding against his self-control.

"Mac, this is crazy." Hilary's voice was breathy and shaken. "We can't do this." She was still pressing against him as she spoke, still offering him that gloriously feminine body in that outrageously sexy green dress. It made it very difficult to take her words to heart.

"What can't we do?" he demanded softly. "This?" His hand slid lower, over her stomach and below. "Or this?" And upward again, to recapture her breast and gently nip its taut center between his fingers. Once again they gasped in unison, both breathing hard.

But she was refusing to give up on the protest she'd raised. "Please listen to me, Mac," she said. He heard the hint of desperation in her voice, and it slowed him somewhat in his headlong plunge into the pleasure of touching her all over. "I can't make love with a man I don't even know."

That made him pause. He'd hoped things weren't going to happen this way, and he wasn't sure what to do now that they had. "You know me," he said slowly.

He felt her shake her head, and saw her glossy black hair sway against her shoulders. "A small piece of you," she said. "I want to know the rest."

His laugh was a short bark. "I'm not so sure you do," he told her. Finally he loosened his grip, and they moved apart slowly.

"Yes, I do," she said. "I have to know, Mac. Who you really are, what you really do. There's a lot more going on here than you've told me, isn't there?"

He had to admit it. "But it's nothing that you need to concern yourself with," he added.

She shook her head again. "Can't you understand, Mac? I'm not like you. I don't take wild and crazy chances. I can't just plunge into things and then pick up and move on to something else."

He looked at her levelly for a moment. She was still breathing quickly, and there was a dark passion in her lovely eyes. "You should try it sometime," he said, only half kidding. "I think you might have a real talent for it."

"What makes you say that?"

The uncertainty in her voice made him step a little closer again. He ran a gentle hand over the curve of her cheek, stopping at her chin. When he tilted her face up to him, he could feel her trembling. "You have a lot of passion behind those deep blue eyes, Hilary Gardiner," he said soberly. "And you can't struggle against it forever, you know."

He could see her struggling against it now. So far it looked like an even match.

"I still meant what I said," she told him stubbornly. "Why won't you tell me what you're really up to?"

He told her the unvarnished truth. "Because I'm afraid that if I do, you'll turn around and walk out on me," he said. "And I don't want that."

"How about this scenario?" she said. "How about you *don't* tell me what's going on, and I turn around and leave."

"Is that a threat, Ms. Gardiner?"

"You bet it is, Mr. MacDougall."

Mac sighed. He was boxed in, and there was no way to get past it. "All right," he said finally. "Let me just get some light, okay?"

Getting out two candles and holders gave him a moment to think. He set the candles up on the card table and lit them. Somehow it felt easier to tell his carefully guarded secrets in the soft glow of the candlelight than it would have been with the overhead lamp on.

"You're not trying to romance your way past this, are you?" she asked him, half smiling.

"No." He pulled up a chair, and sat opposite her. "The romancing comes later."

He couldn't be sure in the dim light, but he thought he saw her blush. *Good.* At least he wasn't the only one in an uncomfortable state.

"If there *is* a later," she reminded him. "So tell me, Mac. Are you really Senator MacDougall's son?"

He nodded. "I really am," he said.

"And you're following in his footsteps, aren't you? With the External Affairs Ministry, I mean."

Another nod. "I didn't intend to," he said. "After I got out of college I was planning to be a journalist. I'd kind of gotten globe-trotting into my system by then, see, because when I was a kid we lived all over the world, wherever my father was posted. I figured as a foreign correspondent I could still travel, but I'd be doing something different from what my father did."

"But . . ." She prompted him when he paused.

"Well, I sort of backed into it. I was visiting my father while he was posted in Cairo, and he told me he needed someone to relay a rather delicate message to someone who might or might not appreciate receiving it. He told me it needed just the right touch—'halfway between a joke and a sermon' was how he phrased it. And then he said I was just the right person to bring it off."

She was watching him thoughtfully, leaning on the table. "I know what he meant," she said. "I've been thinking that ever since I met you. On the surface you're all charm, and all serious purpose underneath."

It bothered him a little to know she'd sized him up so accurately and he hadn't even realized it. "Anyway, that was the start of my career with External Affairs," he said. "It turned out my 'touch' was just what was needed in a lot of situations, and they started finding work for me here and there, all over the world."

"Including Ste. Helene."

"Yes. Ste. Helene actually gets lumped together with some of the other Caribbean islands, since none of them are large enough to have an embassy all of their own. So I was hopping back and forth among them, working on my tan, eating hot food, doing this and that."

He felt his own face set in more serious lines as he remembered the end to that idyllic saga. "I made some good friends there, Hilary. Not all of them survived the coup."

He couldn't read the expression in her large dark eyes. She seemed to be holding off on deciding how she felt about all this.

"My best friend, and a close colleague, was a man named Henry Dubose. He and his wife Sarah were like family to me."

"Sarah? The woman at Domingo's?"

"Yes. I managed to get her out safely with me when I left. But Henry—" His mood darkened as he thought of Henry. He'd heard stories about the new military government's strong-arm tactics. It made him clench his fists whenever he remembered it.

"Is he in trouble?"

"Bad trouble. He found out about the coup just before it happened, and leaked the information to the people who were most at risk. Unfortunately it meant the new government saw him as a traitor, and once they took power, they acted on it. He's under house arrest now, as far as we know."

"House arrest doesn't sound so bad."

"Not unless you know some of the bozos who are guarding him. The only reason he's not in prison is that we've kept up some diplomatic pressure on the government, and they can't afford to ignore that. But he's not safe, as long as he's on the island."

He could see her putting two and two together and coming up with a number she didn't like. "Then those two guys in the car in front of the restaurant—"

"Were watching Sarah, because they suspect she's involved in the effort to get Henry out of Ste. Helene."

"Is she?" The question was blunt. She wasn't enjoying this, Mac could tell.

"No. I wouldn't risk her safety by involving her."

"Are you?"

That was the crux of the matter. Mac gave in to a sigh. "Yes," he admitted. "It's a long story, Hilary, and I can't give even you all the details, but yes, some colleagues and I are working on bringing Henry to Canada, with External's blessing. He was a good friend to us down there, and we feel responsible for the spot he's in now."

Hilary stood up, putting breathing space and thinking space between them. "Tell me how your hot sauce shop is connected to all this," she said.

Mac shifted in his chair, watching her pace to the windows and back. "I needed an excuse to keep up a connection with the island," he said. "That seemed like a convenient one. So far, at least, the Ste. Helenean authorities seem to have bought the line that I'm only interested in their food, not their politics."

"A line you probably made sound halfway between a joke and a sermon," she said.

"However I delivered it, it seems to be working. I have a conduit to some friends down there. When the time comes, we'll seize the opportunity and get Henry out safely."

He half expected her to disapprove, or turn the conversation to the subject of their rival stores. Instead, she asked, "Once he's safe, what will you do?"

The question took him by surprise. "To be perfectly honest, I hadn't planned that far ahead," he said. "I never do. And even if I did, External would probably throw a monkey wrench into it anyway."

"So you'll go back to hopping all over the world."

He stood up, too. She was standing looking out at the city lights through the open French windows. Mac went and stood beside her. "Probably," he admitted. "I guess that sounds crazy to you."

When she turned to look at him, there was an unholy gleam in her eyes. "You want to know something strange?" she said. "Just for a moment, when you were describing it, it didn't sound crazy at all. It actually sounded wonderful." She laughed at herself. "Now *that* sounds crazy, coming from me."

He stepped a little closer, close enough to put his hands on her elbows. He'd shed his tux jacket when they'd sat down, and suddenly all he could think about was getting rid of his white shirt and feeling his skin against hers.

"It *is* wonderful, Hilary." He made his voice as persuasive as he knew how. "It's like a new adventure every day of your life. You've been locked into one route for so long. I wish I could lift you out of that, and show you the whole world."

She laughed again. "Don't tempt me, MacDougall," she said. "I don't know if it's the candlelight or the champagne at the reception or—or what, but just at the moment I'm almost in the mood to take you up on it."

Hilary was astonishing herself, by what she was saying and how she was feeling. The story Mac had told her was so completely outside her experience, so outlandish-sounding, that she felt as though she'd landed in the middle of a spy novel. She was light-headed, not quite sure her feet were firmly planted on the ground.

The way Mac was running his hands over her shoulders wasn't helping her keep a grip on reality, either. She felt herself leaning back against him, floating on a wave that he'd created just for her.

"It's impossible for the two of us to get involved," she whispered. The words were like a lesson she'd memorized without really understanding its meaning.

"Mm-hmm." His murmured agreement was a caress in itself. The sound buzzed softly against her ear, deep and warm.

"We're just too different. We live in completely different spheres." She raised a hand at the nearly empty apartment around her. "I mean, you don't even like *furniture*, for heaven's sake!"

Three things happened then. One was that Mac laughed, and Hilary felt the golden charm of that sound like a breath of sea air in her cautious, landlocked life.

The second thing was that he caught her upraised hand and moved it to his lips. He kissed the very center of it, slowly, seductively, and she felt the brazen eroticism of it right down into the toes of her high-heeled shoes. He tilted her arm and kissed her wrist, connecting with the pulse that beat so close to the surface. He moved lower, burying his face in the crook of her elbow. The masculine scent of him swirled in all her senses like a genie freshly let out of its bottle.

The third and final thing was a thought that came into her head completely unbidden. *Do something just for the moment,* some inner voice prompted her. *Let yourself know what it would feel like to be loved by Mac. Just this once.*

It was contrary to everything she'd learned in life. And maybe that was why it hit her with such sudden and overwhelming force.

She wanted this man. Wanted him in a way she'd never imagined was possible. And he wanted her, could teach her things about loving that she might never have a chance to learn again. Was it really so crazy, when this golden evening was dangling itself right in front of her, to give in to its sensuous charm?

She was a big girl. She knew what she was doing, and she knew it wasn't possible for her to make any kind of a life with Mac. But if they didn't have this night together, she'd spend the rest of her life wondering what making love with him would have been like. This way, she'd know.

Tomorrow she could go back to reality with a clear head, grateful for what they'd shared. A little regretful, perhaps, that it had to end. But free, once and for all, from the question of what might have been.

She shivered with a sudden pleasure that came from deep inside her. She saw Mac look up at her, as if he wondered what was behind the smile on her face.

His voice was husky. "Do you really think my views about furniture are going to get in our way?" he was asking.

She laughed. "I'd like to see them try," she said. She didn't bother to explain why she'd suddenly abandoned her earlier objections. And Mac didn't seem to be in the mood to press the point.

"Good," he said. "Because I do have all the *essential* pieces of furniture, in case you hadn't noticed."

She'd noticed. The double mattress lay in the middle of the wood floor like a centerpiece, inescapable and eye-catching. She'd been so aware of it on her first visit here; now its neatly made surface was like one final temptation to give in to Mac's persuasive appeal.

She ignored the cautious voice that was urging her to spell things out to Mac right now. Somehow it would spoil the magic of the moment if she started making conditions, or checking that he, too, understood that this was a once-only encounter.

Instead, she just smiled at him. "The bed's a little hard to miss, when it's out in the middle of the floor like that," she said. "Do you leave it there to trap unsuspecting women?"

For once, he looked completely serious. "There's only been one woman I've been interested in trapping in recent memory," he said. "And I'm looking at her right now."

Hilary's breath caught in her throat as Mac closed the gap between them and took her in his arms.

Seven

The notion fluttered through Hilary's head that she could actually feel the soft glow of the candlelight on her skin. She moved willingly into Mac's embrace, settling against him with a sigh of pure pleasure.

She felt him start to speak, but then he seemed to change his mind. Maybe he, too, sensed that words had no place here. Instead, he ran his hands searchingly down her back, imprinting her with the tender certainty of his desire for her.

She curved her spine like a contented cat, arching against Mac's body. It was impossible to think beyond this moment, impossible to do anything but revel in their nearness and the way he was touching her. His fingers dug into her waist, urgently, expertly. And then they slid lower.

Hilary let her head fall back, and moaned when he bent to kiss the throbbing base of her neck. How could a man be so hungry and yet so deliberate? The thought of making love with Mac had been tantalizing her since the day they'd met.

Now she was sure it would be even more than she had imagined.

"Hilary..." Her name was the merest whisper. He was kissing her shoulder blades now, driving her wild with the silken movements of his lips and tongue. His voice was languid, husky. "The straps on this dress don't offer much resistance, do they?" She thought she heard a smile in the question.

"I've been thinking that ever since I tried it on." Her words ended in a sudden gasp. Mac pushed aside the tiny straps and the loose bodice of her green gown floated gently down around her waist, leaving her upper body exposed to the warm night air and Mac's tender and erotic touch.

He moved so slowly that Hilary felt as if time was expanding and leaving her floating free of its usual rules. She clasped her hands loosely around his neck, anchoring herself to him. She swayed in his grasp, learning a thousand new ways to feel pleasure while he explored her skin with his hands and his mouth. His touch was everything from feather-soft and casual to muscular and demanding, and every sensation took her a little higher, set her a little bit freer.

"Hilary, it's impossible," he was saying, his lips warm against her skin. "Your skin can't possibly be even softer than I knew it would be."

She tried to frame a bantering remark, intending to ask him how he'd been so darn sure how her skin would feel. But the flippant words wouldn't happen. She couldn't hide what she was feeling. The honesty of her own response astonished her.

"Oh, Mac," she cried, as he covered the lace of her bra with the intimate heat of his mouth. "You're going to drive me crazy if you do that much longer."

The feel of his smile curving against her breast sent lightning ripping right through her. He slid his hands around to her back, and flicked open the hooks of her strapless bra.

Impatient to know where he would take her next, she reached her own hands behind her and shed the sexy scrap of lace.

She vaguely remembered thinking, when she'd put it on, that even though Mac would never see it, she at least felt sexier wearing it. But that had been in another lifetime, when, for some unknown reason, she'd been denying herself the endless spectrum of sensation that Mac was drawing her into now. She let the brassiere fall to the polished wood floor, and undid the zipper in the back of her dress. In a moment it and her stockings were nothing but a small silky pile on the floor.

Mac's eyes were blazing as he watched her. He stood without moving for a moment, and she felt the heat of his gaze, felt the open adoration in it and responded to it more wantonly than she'd have believed possible.

Then he moved, too, rapidly undoing the buttons of his white shirt and shedding it and the rest of his formal evening clothes. They'd both moved without speaking, but Hilary knew her thoughts were as clear to him as his were to her. *These clothes are nothing but a barrier. Let's get rid of them.* Mac's conservative tailored black and white, particularly, was ridiculously out of place. It was like finding a phone booth in the midst of the deepest, darkest jungle. Their loving was something primal and wild, and it had no connection with the polite world they'd left behind.

For a long moment they just looked at each other, eyes locked in an intense stare that made Hilary's breath come even faster. Without shifting her gaze, she was still aware of every masculine detail of him, the broad shoulders that her hands begged to touch, his flat stomach and the seductive line of his hips, the arching proof that he was more than ready to give her the pleasure she was aching for.

Yet it was his eyes that excited her most. They were riveting, hungry, their hazel depths nearly overrun with the blackness of passion.

"You are so lovely," he breathed. "Like a dream—the kind of dream that's so perfect you can never recapture it when you're awake. You are that dream, Hilary."

A shiver snaked its way along the whole length of her spine. She moved with it, involuntarily, and in the same instant Mac stepped forward and pulled her into his arms again.

The meeting of their naked bodies was such a revelation that Hilary was sure her heart stopped beating for a split second. The rightness of it, the incredible sensuousness of her skin against his was a sweet physical jolt.

She heard the wonder and desire in Mac's wordless cry. It was a thousand times more arousing to know that he was finding this just as astonishing as she was. She let herself go then, certain that there was no right or wrong, but only a giving and sharing of pleasure. Fifteen years' worth of caution and inhibition fell away from her like an unnecessary winter coat in the heat of a tropical sun.

His hands were everywhere, following every curve and hollow of her body. And Hilary responded mindlessly. She let her searching palms outline the masculine strength of him, all the lean, aggressive planes that had driven her so wild when she'd seen him a week ago wearing nothing but a bed sheet.

She ran a hand over the hard angle of his shoulders, and felt his muscles shifting fluidly under her fingers when he moved his arms to catch her even more closely against him. The long line of his back was smooth and taut, the round curve of his buttocks more sensually inviting than she would have thought possible.

Every mutual caress was driving them closer to the edge, and when Mac's knowing fingers found the cool, soft skin of her inner thigh and moved upward to where she waited achingly for his touch, Hilary thought she could feel the building sway around her. The hard, intimate pressure of him against her belly had already made her feel she couldn't stand another moment of waiting, but now his caresses were sending her over the brink. She went willingly, propelled by the strength of her need and not caring where it led her.

She heard a voice cry out, and it wasn't until the pulsing inside her had calmed somewhat that she realized she'd been the one responsible for that long, ragged cry. Her breath came unsteadily, and she found herself clinging to Mac's shoulders, wanting to tell him wordlessly how much she loved the new world he was opening up to her.

There was no way to express it. She had to settle for a silent caress, a gentle row of kisses along his heaving collarbone that somehow turned into a long, searching kiss that they both fell into headlong. His mouth was hard and urgent, his movements no longer languid. And in spite of the shuddering climax she'd just experienced, Hilary was still yearning for a greater intimacy, to satisfy the incredible hunger deep inside her.

"It's a good thing we don't have to go looking for your bed," she gasped out.

"Nope." He shifted his weight and found it without looking, by reaching out a foot. "It's right here."

They collapsed onto it gratefully. Hilary felt as though her bones had been flooded by a rippling stream, and Mac's strength was the only thing keeping her on her feet. Only when they were stretched out together, and he was tracing a maddeningly intricate pattern on her breast with his tongue, did a nagging thought from the world of reality intrude itself.

"Mac," she said, not sure how to phrase it. "I never thought—that is, I'm not protected."

He never slowed in his movements. "That's all right," he said. "I am."

She let herself slide back into the warmth of his touch, arching against him when he took her nipple into his mouth. The slippery seduction of his tongue was what finally made it impossible to wait any longer.

"Please," she said, half opening her eyes and watching the tangle of her own fingers in the curly darkness of his hair. "Please, Mac. Make love to me now."

His answering grunt was a refusal with the sound of satisfaction in it. "Not yet," he said. "I haven't finished finding out all about you yet."

Finding out all about her involved a secret exploration with fingers and lips that left Hilary drained and supercharged at the same time. She felt as though she was all nerve endings, all of them startled into surprised life by the thoroughness of Mac's caresses. Who could have known that a kiss placed on the back of her thigh just where the roundness of her buttocks began would make her tremble and moan like a tree in a gale-force wind? There was no end to the discoveries she was making about her own body.

And still she couldn't wait to feel him inside her. She writhed in his grip, propelled by primitive forces. When she shifted against him, encountering the stubborn proof of his own arousal, she knew the time had come.

Something in the way she pressed along the length of him seemed to push him to the edge of his self-control, too. With a final kiss in the soft hollow between her breasts, he abandoned his languid search for the hidden secrets of her body. He moved away briefly, reaching for a small packet Hilary hadn't even noticed at the head of the bed. When he returned to her side, his eyes were serious with the purposeful intensity she found so compelling in him. Raising himself above her, he cradled her between his arms and slid inside her with a long, slow movement that sent Hilary's senses spinning right back into the stratosphere.

When he started to move, it was with a deliberate slowness. But Hilary's need for him was so overpowering now that the idea of pacing things and making this last was far beyond her. She moved against him urgently, propelled by the pounding rhythm in her own body. She was sailing a fast ship on high seas, and all she could do was race with the wind.

Her motions seemed to inflame him. She heard him give a surprised cry, and sensed that his self-control had just scattered into the air. Now they were racing with each other, rocketing toward the horizon where a blinding, blazing sun was waiting for them.

Never, never in her life had she experienced anything like this. Time and place vanished, and the only thing that mattered in the world was this sensation that was beyond pleasure, beyond freedom, beyond everything. She was drowning in it, breathing it in, feeling Mac in every part of her. She was utterly consumed by his loving.

They reached the golden explosion of sunlight together, in one glorious instant. Hilary felt racked with it, possessed by it, for a moment almost unaware of Mac's presence at all. It pounded into her like waves on a hard sand beach, and she reveled in each powerful jolt.

Then, finally, the pounding subsided. She became gradually aware of holding Mac in her arms, and being held by him. His eyes were closed, his hair falling forward over his face. When he slowly opened his eyes to look down at her, there was honest astonishment in their darkened hazel depths.

She reached up to push his hair back, and he smiled faintly. The smile added a new dimension to her feeling of incredible well-being. She could see his usual flippancy struggling to assert itself. But what they'd felt had been more powerful even than laughter, and she knew he was as amazed by it as she was.

For a long time they just lay there, talking slowly, lazily. Mac pulled a sheet over them and they stayed close together under it. The cooling of the night air struck Hilary as a reminder that she'd only surrendered to Mac's seductive charms for this one evening, and even while she lay in his arms, loving the familiar way he was tracing the lines of her shoulder and breast, she knew she was going to have to return to the world outside this nearly empty apartment, and soon.

"What will Todd and Andrew say when you don't come home tonight?" Mac was asking, and that gave her the opening she needed to break the bad news to him.

"I can't stay here, Mac," she said. "Try to understand that."

He was refusing to take it seriously. "I would have said they were old enough to be left on their own, at fourteen," he said. "What do you think they'll be up to?"

She shook her head, and moved slightly away from him. "It's not what they're up to that I'm worried about," she said. "It's what *I'll* be up to, if I let the two of us get any more involved."

She started to get up, but he held her firm with one strong hand. "In my book, it's hard to get any more involved than we just did," he said. "And unless I miss my guess, you felt the same way."

She had to make him understand. She faced him seriously, wishing the soft candlelight didn't make his handsome pirate's face so utterly appealing.

"I've never felt anything quite like that," she said, and hoped her feelings would show in her face, illuminating the words that didn't seem adequate to describe how she'd felt at that dizzying pinnacle of love. "But we have to be realistic about this, Mac. Where on earth could we go with this, if we were crazy enough to continue? After what you just told me about your life tonight, I can't imagine a world any more different from my own."

"What are you saying, lady?"

"That I don't think we should pursue this." There was a sudden lump in her throat as she said the words. It was hard to abandon the golden passion they'd shared.

He lowered his brows. "Then why go this far with it?" he demanded.

"Because I wanted to know." Her rationale didn't seem as solid as it had been an hour ago. "I've never felt so free, Mac, or so alive. I knew you could make me feel that way. I wanted to experience it, just once."

He moved closer to her, trying to recapture her in his arms. "I could make you feel that way every night of your life," he said.

She couldn't help laughing. The laugh was not an amused one. "Where?" she said bluntly. "In Paris one night, and Mozambique the next? I have a family to raise and a business to run, in case you'd forgotten. I can't live my life out of a suitcase, the way you do. Making love to me every night means doing it right here in Ottawa, and somehow I get the feeling you wouldn't enjoy that for long."

His face was stubborn and dark now. "You're being mighty set in your ways, aren't you?" he asked.

"We both are. We're both committed to the lives we have. And it just happens that they don't overlap. That's why I think it's best if we don't go any further with this." She'd thought she could say the words calmly, but her voice kept quivering. She finally freed herself and stepped back into her evening gown. "But this evening will be something I'll always treasure, Mac. Please try to understand that."

He was actually glowering at her now. "Great," he said shortly. "I feel like a stud horse."

His words cut her. "You're being unreasonable," she said. "You just won't admit I have a point."

He put his hands behind his head. Hilary felt a persistent ache inside as she watched the shifting muscles under that smooth warm skin. "You're afraid of getting walked out on again," he said. "So you're killing this before it has a chance to get started."

"Don't tell me what I'm afraid of," she shot back at him. "And since you've never been walked out on, you can't know how it feels."

"How *does* it feel?"

She could hear in his tone of voice that he honestly wanted to know. "It feels like all the supports just gave way," she said. "And it teaches you in a hurry not to trust any support you can't provide for yourself."

"So I'm just another untrustworthy jerk who's bound to let you down, is that it?"

"No." She shook her head at him. "I'm not going to let it get to that point. You're like something out of some big old leather-bound book that has stories about pirates and heroes in it. If I didn't find that exciting as hell, I wouldn't be here now. But you can't ask me to carry that over into my real life. It just won't work."

"We can't just drop this, Hilary."

"We're going to have to. You can live your life any way you please, Mac, but I don't have that luxury." She swallowed past a lump that had lodged in her throat like a sharp-edged stone. "Tonight was very important to me," she added. "Please don't diminish it by trying to hold on to something that never would have worked in the first place."

His wordless snort annoyed her, and that gave her the strength she needed to wrap her shawl around her shoulders and pick up her handbag. Leaving here was far, far harder than she'd thought it would be.

She knew it was because she *hadn't* thought about leaving. She'd thought only about the passion of the moment, and now she was starting to pay for that wonderful sense of abandon. She had a feeling she might be paying for it for quite some time.

"Goodbye, Mac," she said unsteadily. "I hope you pull off that stunt of yours in Ste. Helene."

His only answer was another snort. He seemed deep in thought, and that made her nervous. She'd expected arguments, persuasions, anything but this stubborn silence. After a pause that seemed crammed with a thousand unspoken questions, she finally forced herself to head toward the door.

She was on the point of opening it when she heard Mac's voice behind her.

"Hilary."

"What?" She half turned.

"This isn't over, you know."

"It has to be."

"You can think that if you like. But I'm going to change your mind."

His tone was almost casual, as though they were arguing about something neither of them was very passionate about. And she took the unsettling sound of his voice home with her, where it kept her company during a restless night of half-dreaming, half-waking fantasies.

The day was swelteringly hot. It was Thursday, four days after the Chamber of Commerce reception, and business was not looking up for *Fortissimo*. The heat only made it seem worse, and thoughts of John Augustus Laurier MacDougall weren't helping Hilary's mood any as she and the boys looked over the receipts at the end of the day.

"I think we'll do a bit better this week," Todd said cautiously.

"Maybe you've got a career as a politician ahead of you," Hilary said, looking up at her tall, dark-haired son. "Making overly optimistic projections seems to be a tool of their trade these days."

Todd shook his head. "I told you, I'm going to be an architect," he said. "You wait till you see the new store I design for *Fortissimo* when the place gets successful enough to expand."

Hilary's eyes swam with tears she couldn't, for the life of her, suppress. Todd had wanted to be an architect ever since he was small, and Andrew was equally excited about a career in journalism. For both those things, they would need a university education. The memory of her own years of pushing herself to the limit so that she could raise a family, earn a salary *and* complete a degree came back to her with depressing vividness. She couldn't stand the thought of Todd and Andrew grinding through the same process. But if *Fortissimo* folded, what choice would they have?

She was blinking back the tears and hoping the boys hadn't noticed, when Andrew looked out the window and said casually, "Your pal's here."

Hilary's head whipped around. "What pal is that?" she asked sharply.

Andrew rolled his eyes. "Come on, Mom. You've been moping around like a teenager ever since Saturday night. You know what pal I'm talking about."

"You're a fine one to accuse someone else of being a teenager," she said, but her mind wasn't on the words. She could see him now, swaggering across the sidewalk from where he'd parked that screaming purple motorcycle. And the rakish tilt of his head as he opened her door seemed to suggest that he felt he had a right to be here.

Well, she'd have to straighten him out on that. Her nerves jangled as smartly as the little bells on the door when he stepped inside the store.

"Hello, Mr. MacDougall," she said. "I didn't expect to see you here."

He tossed the boys a smile, and she could sense the complicity in it. "I turn up in all kinds of unexpected places," he said. He was grinning at her now. Damn it, it wasn't fair. She could resist almost anything but that free-spirited laughter in his eyes.

"Got any plans for dinner?" he was asking.

She was startled enough that she told him the truth without planning to. "We hadn't thought that far ahead yet," she said.

He nodded. She had the sneaking feeling he already knew that, and a sidelong look at Todd and Andrew made her think they had something to do with it. Had this under-handed buccaneer actually gone as far as enlisting her own sons on his side? Well, she'd always known he played by his own rules.

"Good thing I have a picnic all ready, then, isn't it?" he said cockily. "Got anyplace in mind that you'd like to eat?"

Hilary managed a shaky laugh. "Why do I have the suspicion you already have one picked out?" she asked.

"Because you're learning how I operate. In fact, I have a favorite picnic spot over in the park, in Hull. It'll be about ten degrees cooler than it is here. Ready to go?"

Hilary looked helplessly at the three of them. Todd and Andrew were wearing grins all too reminiscent of Mac's own.

"I have to drop the cash at the bank," she said. "I suppose we could go once I've done that." She leveled a forefinger at Mac. "But there's no need to look so smug about it, MacDougall."

His satisfied smile only widened. Hilary had the uncomfortable feeling that she'd just been shanghaied, and there wasn't a thing she could do about it.

They ate hot chicken wings and cold potato salad in a quiet shady spot Mac knew in Gatineau Park. The big park's lower reaches came right down into the city of Hull, Ottawa's neighbor across the river, and made Hilary feel she'd gotten completely away from the heat and the pavement even though they were practically within sight of the city.

She felt herself lapsing into a dangerous relaxation with Mac around. He made her laugh, and she couldn't help responding to that. She couldn't help entering into the spirit of things when he challenged the boys to add some more hot sauce to their chicken wings. Todd tried manfully to cover up his response to the flaming stuff Mac dumped on his dinner, and Andrew collapsed in mock agony in the third round of competition. When Mac turned to Hilary, humor and perception glinting in his hazel eyes, she astonished all three of them by slathering the wing she held in the hottest sauce Mac had provided, and then eating it demurely. Andrew groaned.

"Obviously your taste buds were burned away long ago," he said. Hilary just smiled.

The more laughter they shared, the harder it was to remember why she'd been so adamant about wanting Mac out of her life. She was fighting the familiar stirrings of desire that his closeness always created, even though he made no move to touch her, and even refused her offer of a ride to and from the park in her car. He insisted on riding by himself, and when they said good-night after Mac had packed up the remains of the feast, Hilary was no closer to knowing what was in his mind than she had been when he'd shown up at the store hours earlier.

She didn't find out on Sunday, either, because most of the day was taken up with a trip to Montreal to see a baseball game. He'd called on Saturday night and caught her stewing over the state of *Fortissimo*'s ledgers. Her concern for the store had made her abrupt with him at first. She'd reminded herself that if it weren't for Mac's crazy scheme to rescue his friend in Ste. Helene, her own store would probably be turning a reasonable profit by now.

But his easygoing voice had somehow gotten around her worries, and she'd found herself agreeing to the trip to Montreal with what felt suspiciously like eagerness. This was nuts, she told herself. She was just avoiding the moment when she and Mac would have to face facts. But something about the lazy warmth of summer, or the intense pleasure she always felt when they were together, was making her put off the painful deed.

They went kite flying one evening, and she found herself laughing like a child with the delight of it. The brightly colored kite Mac had brought for her tugged at the string in her hands as if it was begging to be let loose on the wind. She felt a crazy empathy with it, and an irrational need to let it free.

She was cautious enough not to invite him to her home, and he seemed to understand that. Letting him into her everyday world would be too much like looking into the future, when she knew they had none. But when he asked her if she'd like to go to Domingo's with him one evening for dinner, she said yes, and dressed in her favorite summer outfit for the occasion. In the bright white of a loosely floating cotton dress, she felt clean and young and alive, and all those things she *hadn't* felt in the years before Mac had come into her life.

Over dessert and coffee in the courtyard, she let down her guard enough to say, "You've never mentioned what happened that evening at your house."

His gaze was direct. "Thought I'd wait for you to bring it up," he said.

"Are you hoping for it to happen again?"

He shrugged, a trifle too lazily. The shrug gave him away. He was as watchful as she was herself, waiting to see where all of this might lead. "Nothing would make me happier," he said. "But I thought we'd take it one step at a time."

"The first step being picnics and kite flying and dinner out," she said thoughtfully.

"No." He leaned forward in his chair. "The first step is to remind you that the two of us are good together, too good to turn our backs on."

She felt a sudden twist in her gut. He was right, but that still didn't answer any of the questions. "And once we've established that, what next?" she asked.

He shrugged again. "I told you, this is a very deliberate process. I hadn't thought ahead to Step Number Two yet."

The deceptive calm of their being together was close to shattering, Hilary knew. They couldn't act as though they were starting from the beginning. The torrent of longing they'd given in to at Mac's apartment was still there, for both of them. And the memory of that white-hot passion could not be ignored.

"You haven't touched me, not since that night." Her words came out in a near-whisper.

"No." His voice was as low as her own. "And I'm planning to collect a whole lot of saint-and-martyr points for that, too, when I get to heaven."

"Does that mean you've wanted to?"

He reached for her hand where it lay on the small table, and captured it with his own. His skin was as smooth and warm as she remembered, and as intoxicating. She could feel the pounding of his blood where his fingertips met her wrist.

"What do you think?" he asked quietly.

She heard the quiver of desire in that low voice, and her whole body responded to it with something that was exactly halfway between joy and anguish. They were right back where they'd started, and she still didn't have the first idea what to do about it.

"Thanks. I'll be around to see you tomorrow at about two, then." Hilary hung up the phone and turned to face her friend Karen. In Karen's face she could see the same anxiety that was tying knots in her own stomach.

"What did he say?" Karen asked.

"He thinks it's not out of the question. He did point out that banks are pretty conservative when it comes to funding businesses that don't have a proven track record. And at this point, *Fortissimo* doesn't look great as an investment."

She sighed as she looked around the small shop. It *looked* so cheerful, with its bright rows of bottles lining the walls and the brilliant reds and oranges of the display she and Karen had just finished setting up in the front window. Her sauces, however, weren't the only things that were red. There was far too much red ink in the ledger books, and she'd finally taken the dreaded step of making a date with her bank manager to see if she could buy herself some time. When she thought of how carefully she'd planned this venture, and the love and expertise she'd poured into it, she wanted to cry.

"It's just until Mac closes out," Karen pointed out. "Once he's gone, things should start looking up in a hurry."

No doubt Karen thought she was being comforting, but Hilary felt a spasm of pain inside whenever she thought about it. Karen was absolutely right, from a business point of view. But even if *Fortissimo could* hang on until Mac's Hot Stuff closed next spring, she knew she'd only be facing another kind of heartache. Mac would be gone, off sailing the seven seas again, and she knew no amount of financial success would ease the hurt of that.

"That's assuming we can last out the year," she said to Karen. "The way things have been going this week, I'm beginning to wonder if that's even possible. There hasn't been a single person in here so far today."

As if to prove her wrong, the bells on the door jingled to announce the welcome arrival of a customer. The man seemed in a hurry, but very eager to have some hot barbecue sauce. Hilary sold him three bottles of it, and was just wrapping them up when the door opened again.

This time it was a woman who said she understood Hilary had something that might be used as a substitute for Ste. Helenean curry sauce. Hilary glanced at Karen, sharing her friend's puzzled look, and went to the shelves to help the woman pick out a curry sauce that would go well with chicken.

The day picked up from there. For the first time since opening day, there was a steady stream of customers, several of whom said how glad they were to find out about her, and how attractive the store was.

At first Hilary had the vague idea that this was just the answer to her deeply felt prayers. But by later in the afternoon, when Todd and Andrew came by to help her close up, she was wondering if there was something else behind it.

"Care for a quick trip down to Byward Market?" she asked them, knowing her two "spies" were always game for an expedition. "I'm wondering if there's something going on at Mac's that I should know about."

They were gone in an instant, and back by the time she was getting the day's deposit ready. She was carefully counting the day's receipts—actual money, and lots of it— when the boys returned.

"Well, we *think* it's good news," Todd said.

"But we're not sure," Andrew added.

Hilary looked sharply at them. "Care to be more specific?" she said.

Andrew pulled a crumpled piece of paper out of his pocket and smoothed it against the surface of the counter. "His place was locked up tight," he said. "But there was a note on the door. I copied it down."

He cleared his throat and read. " 'Gone out of town unexpectedly. Sorry to inconvenience anyone. Great hot sauce also available at *Fortissimo.*' And then he gives the address."

Hilary sat down rather suddenly on the stool behind the counter. "Well, that explains the customers," she said.

She thought of the gratifying jingling of the bells on the door every time a new customer had walked in. Thanks to Mac's note, she was putting real cash in the bank for the first time in weeks.

But like everything else about the man, the answer was even more complicated than the question. She couldn't run a business by picking up Mac's leavings whenever he had to go out of town unexpectedly. And the busy day today only pointed out more graphically how much better his store was doing than hers.

Worse yet, she had a feeling she knew where he'd gone. It was all very well to joke about her two boys playing spies, but Mac was doing it in real life. Could she even contemplate a future with a man who disappeared at the drop of a hat to go charging off on God knew what improbable and possibly dangerous trip?

She knew she couldn't. She looked sadly at the piles of cash and cheques in the drawer, and then smiled wanly at her boys. "Thanks for the information," she told them. "And you're absolutely right. I have no idea whether it's good news or not."

Eight

Mac had never really understood the phrase "bone-weary." Tonight he did. Every part of him ached, and he knew it wasn't just that he'd had almost no sleep in the previous two nights, or the fact that he'd failed in his attempt to get Henry off of Ste. Helene in the past two weeks.

It was more than those things. It was coming home alone, opening his apartment door and having the open, empty room seem bare and unwelcoming for the first time since he'd moved in here.

Hell, he'd *never* been bothered by coming home alone to empty rooms. He'd been doing it all his adult life. Yet here he was standing in his own doorway, reluctant to go inside because he suddenly didn't feel at home here.

This was ridiculous. Of course he wasn't at home here. He wasn't really at home anywhere. That was how he liked things. He liked the feeling of being free to float with the wind, wherever the Ministry of External Affairs or his own fancy wafted him. It was just those two nearly sleepless nights that were making him feel this way tonight.

He walked in and clicked on the light, and knew he was wrong. The place *did* seem too empty. He *didn't* want to be here alone. With a sudden, brutal burst of honesty, he admitted to himself that he wanted to come home and have Hilary waiting for him. He wanted her to be here, now.

The idea shocked him right down to his socks.

He made himself unpack the minimal things he'd taken with him. He poured himself a beer, noticing that three more beers and a jar of peanut butter were the only occupants of his refrigerator. He thought about going out to eat, but dismissed the idea. He sat on his balcony and drank his beer and watched the fairy-tale lights of the Parliament Buildings reflecting softly in the moving surface of the river.

He thought about the way Hilary's face had looked when she'd left him, that night after the reception. He pictured the shining dark wave of her hair, and the dark blue jewels that were her eyes. He closed his own eyes and conjured up the expression she'd worn.

Calm certainty, clouded by regret. The smoky remnants of the passion they'd vaulted themselves into. And something else. Something that had been haunting him for the past two weeks.

It was something like hope. Mac had a sneaking feeling, deep down in his weary bones, that Hilary wanted to be able to trust again. She'd buried that hope under a lot of layers. But maybe the vibrant force of their lovemaking had teased it back up near the surface. And maybe if it happened once, it could happen again.

He had to know. The shock of coming home and realizing he wanted to walk in the door to Hilary's smiling face was enough to make him want to throw the habits of a lifetime overboard.

He took a deep breath and got to his feet with a sudden jerk. Back inside, he headed straight to the phone. He punched out Hilary's number and held his breath, feeling as if he'd just jumped out of a moving vehicle. He'd either end up with a broken limb or find himself standing firmly on the ground, depending on the kind of welcome she gave him.

At first it was a tentative one. "Back in town?" she said casually, and he couldn't tell what, if anything, she meant by that.

"Just got in about half an hour ago. I meant to call you before I left, but there wasn't time. I had about five minutes to stick a sign on my door, grab a toothbrush and get to the airport."

"That's all right."

What was behind her carefully neutral tone? He had to know. "Aren't you going to ask me where I went?" he said.

"I think I can guess. You were on Ste. Helene, weren't you?"

"Yes."

"Did you have any luck?"

"No. Not a damn bit of it." He sat down at his card table and leaned his elbows on it, tiredly. "Hilary, is there any chance in the world of seeing you tonight?"

There was a long pause. "You know, I've just spent two weeks going over all the perfectly good reasons why you and I shouldn't see each other anymore," she said.

"Convince yourself?"

"Partly."

"Could I speak with the part that isn't convinced, please?"

He heard a faint chuckle. "Speaking," she said.

"Good. Hilary, I'm sitting here alone in this big empty place and the only thing I can think of is being with you. Let the boys spend an evening on their own, and come on over here."

"Actually, the boys are away this weekend. They always spend Labor Day weekend with their father in Toronto."

So far, Mac hadn't thought too highly of the absent Skip Gardiner and the way he'd walked out on Hilary and the boys. Now he felt himself positively liking the guy.

"Is that so? So you're on your own."

"Yes."

"Does that mean yes, you'll come and see me?"

The pause was even longer this time. "I'm not sure that's such a great idea."

"Had a change of heart about me in the past two weeks?"

"Let's just say I've been thinking about things a little more clearly."

"Sounds grim."

He swore he could hear her smile. "What *have* you been up to, Mac?"

"Come on over here, and I'll tell you."

He pictured her, fiercely. His mind's eye ran over the dark sheen of her hair and the creaminess of her skin, and delivered him a verdict: this impossibly young-looking mother was a woman who'd been robbed. An early mistake and a self-centered man had taken away half the life that should have been hers.

And he, Mac, was going to give it back to her. He wasn't sure just how, yet. He just knew he had to see her, to have her close to him again.

He leaned his forehead on the heel of one hand and closed his eyes. His imagination shimmered with images of her, unclothed and as white as a tropical beach.

"Listen to me," he said, with sudden urgency. "This can be a purely social call, if you like. I'm not planning to turn it into a great seduction scene, if that's what you're thinking. The way I feel at the moment, I'm not sure I could pull it off, even if I tried."

He heard her chuckle again. "Tired?" she asked.

"Tired, cubed. And I've just spent two weeks acting cheerful when I wasn't, and pretending I was interested in one thing when it was something completely different I had on my mind. I'm tired of putting up a front." He held on to the phone a little harder. "I can't pretend with you, anyway. Never wanted to."

He could sense her weighing, considering. Had she ever, since her disastrous early marriage, just acted on the spur of the moment and damned the consequences?

He knew she had. It had happened right here, in his big lonely apartment. For one glorious evening, the apartment hadn't been lonely and Hilary hadn't been careful and cautious.

And because of that one evening, she was being even more careful now. Mac cursed himself for letting things get beyond his control so soon, and knew at the same moment that he'd do it all exactly the same way if the occasion arose again.

"Well?" Hunger for her was making him impatient.

"A purely social call, you said."

"If that's what you want."

"Believe me, it is. All right, I'm on my way. And Mac?"

"Yes?"

"This may sound crazy, but I missed you."

The knot inside him loosened a little. "I think that's the sanest thing you've said so far. And I missed you, too. God, did I miss you!"

He added the last phrase after she'd hung up. He stood there listening to the buzz of the dial tone for half a minute, as though it might tell him what the hell he should do next.

Shave, it seemed to be saying. He hadn't had a chance to clean up properly before his flight back here. He headed for the bathroom and had just had time to shower and shave when he heard the doorbell ringing.

Hilary didn't usually get into this state. Usually she spelled things out very carefully for herself, and charted her course accordingly. Usually she knew what was the sensible thing to do, and she did it.

The trouble with Mac was, she didn't know if falling in love with him was a sensible thing or not. His jetting around on mysterious missions made her very, very nervous. But then, the mere sound of him on the telephone could make her laugh. When she was around him she didn't know whether to kick against his hellion's charm or jump up and down for sheer lightheartedness.

"Light-headedness is more like it," she grumbled to herself as she stood on his doorstep.

One thing was very clear to her. Making love with Mac hadn't cleared anything up, and it certainly hadn't gotten him out of her system. If anything, he'd managed to become even more firmly lodged in her life since their night together.

No matter what else happened between them tonight, she was *not* going to let passion take over again. That hadn't solved anything.

It was easy to say, until the door opened and she found herself facing that enticing male body of his, wearing jeans and nothing more. Her breathing constricted at the strength of him. At the hard, lean hips. The tousled hair, damp and slicked back from his face.

It wouldn't stay there, she knew. It would dry and curl and fall back over his forehead and tease her the way so many things about him teased and distracted her. The light in his hazel eyes. His long, agile fingers. That ready grin.

The grin looked a bit shopworn tonight. She followed him upstairs, noting that his step was heavier than usual, and the set of his shoulders not so carefree. "You do look tired, Mac," she said, when he closed the door behind them. "I remember how exhausting it can be, keeping up a cheerful face for somebody else's benefit."

He eyed her carefully. "Didn't know you'd ever been in my line of work," he commented.

"I haven't. But pretending to two little boys that everything is all right when you're actually down to your last hundred bucks in the world amounts to the same thing, as far as I can tell."

He gave a short laugh. "Sure sounds like it," he said. Then his eyes narrowed. "Are you telling me that for a reason, Ms. Gardiner?"

"It's possible. I don't want us to get carried away again, like we did before. I want things to be very clear between us, because if they aren't . . ." She let the sentence trail.

"If they aren't, then what?"

She might have known he wouldn't let her get away with being so vague. The trouble was, things *weren't* very clear between them, and she didn't know how to make them clear.

She backed up and started again. "Maybe I just wanted to interject a note of common sense into all this," she said.

"All this?" He raised an eyebrow at her. His hair was starting to dry already, and she could see the first curl getting ready to droop down toward that cocky eyebrow. She shoved her hands into the pockets of her white sundress, to keep them from getting any ideas about pushing that wayward curl back up again.

"You know what I mean, MacDougall. This situation we're in. Whatever you call it."

Something strange was happening to her. She'd felt it before around Mac, but never this strongly. She had the utterly irrational feeling that the floor was tilting under her feet, and that the warm summer breeze coming in from the open French doors had the taste of salt to it.

It was all because of the way he was looking at her. His eyes were serious, strangely haunted, almost all trace of joking gone. *Almost.* That lingering bit of a smile reached out to her as surely as if he'd been touching her.

"What do I call it? I'll tell you what I call it." The smile strengthened, transformed his face into something satisfied and hungry all at the same time. "I call it falling in love," he said.

The ship gave a sudden lurch. Or maybe it was Hilary's knees, buckling on her. She realigned herself, grabbing at common sense, and stood up tall as she got ready to set him straight.

"Oh, no, Mac," she said firmly. "Falling in love is the last thing in the world you and I are going to do."

He seemed to be enjoying her protest. At least, the smile in his eyes was catching on, crinkling those little lines on his face that told her about all the hair-raising adventures that had shaped his past, and determined his future.

It was those same hair-raising adventures that made her so determined not to give her heart to him. A part of her cried out *But you already have,* and she felt herself being buffeted and tilted again, from within this time.

Her high-handed buccaneer was cad enough to echo her own thoughts. "Your English isn't as fluent as I thought," he said, grinning outright now. "You were using the future tense just then. I don't think falling in love is something we're *going* to do, Hilary. I think we're well on our way to doing it already."

She shook her head. "No," she said. "We're not."

She expected a glib torrent of persuasive words. He gave her something different, something that only heightened her impression that the room was shifting under her feet.

He came close to her, standing slightly behind her so they were both looking out the tall French doors to the hazy late-summer night outside. She stiffened, anticipating his touch and trying to fight off her own longing for it.

He didn't touch her. He just stood there.

"Just" was the wrong way to put it. He managed to surround her with the warm haze of his physical presence without moving a muscle. She was primitively aware of his nearness, and the heat of his naked upper body. Her breathing shifted up a gear, without her meaning to.

"I think you're wrong," he said softly.

She heard his voice as a tangible thing, a velvety expanse that she couldn't help wanting to run her hands over. She asked him a question, but her mind wasn't completely on his answer. Mostly she just wanted to roll herself in that velvet voice again.

"What are you trying to do, Mac?"

He chuckled. "Just get you to admit what's really going on, that's all," he said.

Hilary closed her eyes. Against all the odds, he was doing it to her again. She was caught in the undertow, dragged—willingly, worse yet—into the deep waters where colored fish swam and wonders happened, wonders she hadn't allowed herself to contemplate for most of her adult life.

She fought against it. She'd given in to this exotic persuasion once before. Letting herself succumb to the magic a second time would only complicate things further.

So she stood, and waited, and felt herself trembling. It was like being hooked up to a low-voltage current. She felt invaded, crowded in on.

She loved it. That was the worst of all. There was such intense pleasure in the way she quivered inside. She remembered the way she'd pulsed and floated when they made love. Her skin recalled every shining sensation of it, and deep down inside there were treacherous parts of her urging her to repeat the experiment, just in case she'd forgotten any of it along the way.

Mac lifted his hands, with palms reaching toward her shoulders. He stopped an inch shy of actually touching her. The anticipation of his touch was one kind of jolt to her system, but it was even more jarring to have that touch withheld.

"So what you're saying is that you'd rather I didn't touch you, right?" She heard the teasing in his tone, and also a note of gruffness, as though he were having his own problems fighting back a voice that told him to go ahead.

"I think it would be better if you didn't."

"Better, eh?"

Those knowing hands came a fraction of an inch closer. Hilary's head tilted back, and a gale-force gust shook her body.

"*Much* better." Even her voice was shaking now.

She knew he'd noticed it, and knew it pleased him. He was standing half behind her, just beyond her range of vision. But she was sure he was grinning, the smug son of a gun. She wanted to make him stop. And she didn't want him ever to stop.

"And kissing you would be right out of the question, I guess."

Mock-regret in his voice. A surprising hint of tenderness, too. And behind it all, the roughness of passion suppressed. There was enough sexual energy zinging around the room to blow a fast clipper ship all the way from the old world to the new, Hilary thought blindly.

"Kissing me would be—" *Wonderful* was the word that sprang to mind. But that would be it, right there. "Out of the question," she finished, falling back on his own teasing words.

"Too bad." He lowered his head, closer to her bare neck and then a little closer yet. She felt herself tensing, her whole body begging silently for him to complete the caress this time. What kind of sainthood certification did a woman have to achieve before she was proof against this kind of temptation? Hilary didn't want to know.

She *did* want him to touch her. She couldn't help it. She leaned back slightly, aching to meet the warmth of his mouth on her neck.

She felt it—a glancing kiss, as warm as a trade wind, as brief as the flash of foam on the crest of a wave. She heard herself give a wordless cry, a gasp that admitted with naked honesty just how much she was longing for him. For a glorious instant his hands closed over her bare shoulders, holding her, rocking her with the intensity of his closeness and strength.

And then he lifted his head again. His hands unclenched themselves from her shoulders, leaving her shaking in every muscle and alive in each and every nerve ending. He could have touched her anywhere at that moment and her response would have been just as wild and hungry.

It wasn't right that a man should be able to dismantle her resolve piece by little piece like this. It wasn't right, but it was irresistible. And if the darkness of desire in his voice and the unsteady sound of his breathing was any indication, she'd managed to take him apart just as devastatingly.

"Good thing we're not going to do any of that, isn't it?" he asked her.

Now was the moment. She could turn and face him, knowing with utter certainty that those strong arms would close around her and pull her into the circle of his loving. She knew, now, just how he could rock the foundations of her whole being, and it was agonizingly tempting to let him do it again.

She closed her eyes tightly. She willed the picture of her house to come into her mind, and finally, it did. She pictured its subdued gray stucco and the carefully tended shrubs at the front. She saw her two nearly grown sons heading up the front steps, coming home to dinner. She envisioned her store, with its carved wood sign announcing its presence to the world.

That safe, contented life of hers was on a direct collision course with the one Mac was tempting her into. And she'd worked so hard and so long to make things safe and contented. She wouldn't—couldn't—let it all disappear.

Finally she summoned up the strength to step away from Mac's explosive closeness. She could almost hear the wrench it took for her to do it. She turned to face him from a safe distance of several feet away, and said pointedly, "If I didn't know better, I'd say you were trying to seduce me."

"If I didn't know better, I'd say I damn near succeeded." His voice was hoarse now, all traces of joking gone. Against the worn front of those old jeans, she could see the unmistakable evidence of his desire for her. The electric hum in her veins intensified as she looked at him, and the realization crowded in on her that she was never going to be quite safe with this man, no matter how levelheaded she tried to be.

"What changed your mind?" he was asking.

She hauled in a deep breath. It didn't calm that electric buzz, but it did get some badly needed oxygen into her system. "My own better sense," she said. "It goes pretty deep with me, I'm afraid."

"So I noticed." He moved, too, as if motion was some sort of release. He went to the refrigerator and took out two beers, holding them up to her silently. She nodded, and he got an extra glass out of the minimally stocked cupboard.

It wasn't until they were sitting out on the balcony, chairs safely at opposite ends of the small porch, that Hilary spoke again. "Tell me about what happened on Ste. Helene," she said.

"There's not much to tell. I got a tip that the guard on Henry's house was going to be changed, and that we might be able to fool the military into hiring one of our own people for the duty. But it turned out to be just a rumor. Too bad I wasted two weeks finding that out."

"Mac, tell me something."

"What's that?"

"Quite honestly, does this have the potential to be dangerous for you?"

Up until now, she'd allowed the thought of Mac putting himself in danger to lie restlessly at the back of her mind, frightening but vague. Now it seemed important to know for certain.

"Could be," he said briefly.

"In what way? I mean, could you be—well, arrested or anything?"

He gave a short laugh. "Security forces on Ste. Helene don't waste much time arresting people these days," he said. "Henry is an exception, of course. But a lot of other people haven't had the luxury of house arrest, or even a prison cell."

He was talking about being killed. For sweet heaven's sake, the man was sitting there calmly on a balcony in quiet, diplomatic Ottawa and admitting calmly that there could be a bullet waiting for him the next time he went to Ste. Helene. And she had no doubt that there would be a next time.

"Of course," he was continuing, with that breezy confidence she found so alluring and so maddening, "it all depends on how cautious I choose to be. This past trip, I was being pretty careful, because I had a feeling that the tip we got wasn't top quality."

The very idea of Mac charging into one volatile situation after another made Hilary's insides quaver with projected dread. But she couldn't leave the subject alone; it had a forbidden fascination for her. This was the part of Mac she couldn't ever share, the part that made it impossible for them to be together. She had to know as much as he would tell her about it.

"Why did you go, if you didn't trust the tip?" she asked.

He seemed reluctant to tell her. "It had something to do with *Fortissimo*," he said slowly.

"I don't understand." She looked at him blankly.

"It's been tearing me up to know that my crazy scheme to run a store for a year could mean bankruptcy for you," he said. "I've been trying like hell to think of a way to get around it, and when we got this message from Ste. Helene, I thought *Great*. Here's a way to wrap this whole business up in a hurry, liquidate my store and leave Hilary all the

customers to herself. It seemed like a good idea at the time,"
he added, half apologetically.

He wasn't smiling now, and neither was she. A dozen
thoughts chased each other around in her head, gratitude for
Mac's concern being chief among them. The question of
what would have happened if he'd succeeded in Ste. Helene
ran a close second.

His hazel eyes rested on her face, watching her, questioning. Hilary knew she had to respond somehow. She grabbed
the reply that was uppermost in her swirling thoughts at that
moment.

"Once you *do* get Henry off the island, what will you do
next?" she blurted out.

He waved the question away. "I never count my plots before they're hatched," he said. "I've developed a few superstitions over the years, Hilary. And one of them is never
to assume I'm going to succeed in something, until I've actually done it."

Hilary had a few superstitions of her own. The major one
had to do with handsome, charming men who swept you off
your feet and then swept out of your life again, leaving you
high and dry. The adolescent love she'd felt for Skip had had
none of the depth and passion of what she and Mac had
shared, but it had still hurt like the devil when Skip had left.
How much worse would she feel when Mac resumed his far-
flung career and left her here in Ottawa?

She was struggling against the idea, struggling to protect
what was left of the layers of insulation around her heart.
She focused desperately on details, because it hurt too much
to look at the big picture.

"This goes far beyond a job with you, doesn't it?" she
said. "You really care about Henry."

He gave her a sharp look, but nodded. "Sarah and Henry
treated me like family when I lived down there," he said.
"They made me feel at home."

Hilary cast a backward look into the big, bare apartment. "This, from a man who boasts about living out of a suitcase?" she said.

He dragged a hand over his eyes. "Sounds wrong, doesn't it? I'm not sure how to explain this to you, Hilary, but something's been changing for me in the past few months. Maybe it started with Sarah and Henry, or maybe it happened when I got back to Ottawa and discovered that I didn't seem to know how to settle down. Or maybe—" He looked directly at her now, and she felt the burning heat of his hazel eyes. "Maybe it has something to do with you."

She resisted the urge to say *With me?* Resisting the urge was made easier by the fact that she seemed to have lost the power to speak temporarily.

"When I walked in that door tonight, you know what my first thought was?"

"That you wanted a beer?" Her voice had more than a hint of frog in it.

"I'm serious, Hilary. Serious, for once. My first thought was that I wanted to be coming home, opening a door and finding you on the other side of it. And that's God's honest truth."

She was out of her chair like a startled deer. This couldn't be happening, she told herself. Here was the man who'd been haunting her dreams with his cocky, break-the-rules grin, the man she'd fallen in love with—she might as well admit it, since he'd pushed her to the point—here he was inviting her into a world where she knew she had absolutely no place. She clutched the balcony rail and prayed for sanity.

"Did you give any thought to how you were going to arrange to have me on the other side of all those doors?" she asked. There was a whole chorus of frogs in her throat now. "Or was it my door you were envisioning opening?"

"I thought we could work those details out," he said.

"How?"

Her one blunt word got him to his feet, too. He moved to her side, one gesture away from pulling her into his arms. She held herself stiffly, trying to counteract that pull of desire.

"If we admit we want each other, we'll find a way to do it," he said stubbornly.

Hilary shook her head. "You're offering me moonshine, Mac," she said. "I need concrete answers."

"What's wrong with moonshine? I love the way it goes to my head. I thought you did, too."

He stepped a little closer. Hilary edged away, desperately trying not to muddy her thinking with the sweet torrent of feeling she knew would flood over her if she let herself fall into his arms.

"Moonshine doesn't provide dinner for two voracious boys every evening," she told him. Her voice pleaded with him to understand. "It doesn't help run a business. It doesn't cut any ice with importers and customs brokers. It won't help much when we're tired and angry with each other about something and you want to take off and I want to stay home. It won't *last,* Mac."

There was green fire in his eyes now. "You're writing this off because you've never gotten over being ditched by Biff or Jeffy or whatever his name is," he said.

"His name is Skip." Her tone was tight. "And I'm not writing this off."

It seemed so important to make him understand that. She turned to face him, and was caught by the blaze in his eyes. Without meaning to she raised her hands to his chest, and felt his arms close around her.

Her next words were muffled against the warm skin of his chest. "Writing this off is the last thing on earth I want to do. I just think we have to apply some common sense to the problem, that's all."

She felt his laughter against her cheek. The curling hairs on his torso were like a million small caresses.

"Common sense won't lift the top of your head clean off, the way mine always feels when I see you," he told her. His voice was husky and near, lapping her in its resonant warmth. "It won't make your heart pound, or your blood sing. You need moonshine for that, Hilary."

She exhaled deeply, and let herself sink farther into his embrace. "Think there's any chance of my common sense and your moonshine getting together on this?" she asked softly.

His reply was a soft chuckle that seemed to vibrate right through her frame. She knew it wasn't the definitive answer she'd been hoping for, knew too that they hadn't really gotten any closer to that answer tonight.

Except that they'd admitted what they felt for each other, and acknowledged its power. That seemed enough for now.

It was enough to lift her heels from the floor as she raised herself up to meet his lips. She had that unsettling feeling of swaying again, although he held her tight in the strong circle of his arms. She answered his kisses urgently, almost hungrily. His mouth was soft and dark and knowing, his tongue demanding a response and delightedly welcoming the sudden abandoned wave that seemed to sweep over her.

Her mind was tossing images at her out of the chaos. She heard a clock running, and it spurred her on to even more frantic caresses, as if this heady freedom had a time limit on it and might be gone before she'd explored it fully.

At the same time, she was grasping at the notion that maybe there *was* a future for her and Mac after all. It beckoned, teased, lured her from a hiding place just out of her sight. That, too, drove her on.

She didn't know which image to follow. In the end she abandoned them both, and gave herself up to the silver and gold sensations of Mac's hands outlining her body through the cotton of her dress, and his lips plundering hers as though he'd found a well of cool, sweet water after a long dry season.

She was remotely aware of shifting position when he bent slightly and slid one hand under her bare knee. It seemed so natural to be swung up into his strong grip, cradling against his chest, letting her arms circle his neck. Her head rested on his shoulder, and he kissed her through the screen of her hair. She shivered convulsively inside at the picture of his curving, smiling lips against that shining blackness.

The French doors were open to let the evening breeze into the heat of the big room inside. Mac strode into the apartment with Hilary still in his arms, heading straight for the mattress that was still the centerpiece of the barely furnished place. He dropped to his knees, letting her stretch slowly onto the bed, and then he lay beside her.

"Pretty good quality moonshine you brew up here," she murmured. How could she feel so languid when passion was ripping through her like a rushing wave? She smiled lazily at him, and saw herself reflected in the near-blackness of his eyes.

"Thanks." His voice was low and husky. "We aim to please."

He aimed to do a darn sight more than just please. Pleasure was only the starting point: before they'd even finished shedding their clothes Hilary was loose with wanting, lost in a sea of touch and sensation. She caressed him with a sureness and a subtlety she'd have sworn she didn't possess, and cried out wildly over and over as Mac's hands and lips ravaged every shred of her self-control.

By the time he buried himself inside her she was a wild woman, half drunk with the powerful knowledge of her own femininity and the realization of what it could do to a man. No, not *a* man, but this one man, who'd unmasked her so devastatingly. Body and soul, she wanted him.

She was more than his match in passion and hunger tonight. She let herself be carried away with the escalating rhythm he set, and drove them both on to a heady climax with as much abandon as if she'd never planned or pondered a consequence in her life.

The shattering of their separate worlds was wildly unexpected and explosively satisfying. Hilary found herself sobbing out Mac's name, clinging to him as she waited for her eyes to focus again. Her vision seemed to have wandered off on its own, and she'd seen the universe stripped naked, gleaming silver and gold like the sun reflecting off a wind-ruffled sea. She'd been shocked by the tumultuous light show behind her own eyelids.

She'd thought she already knew what wonders making love with Mac could reveal. But this was new, and utterly astonishing. Was is possible for them to create a different kind of magic, a new and startling revelation, each time they loved?

High-quality moonshine, indeed!

Nine

She never intended to spend the night. It just happened, as naturally as their lovemaking had happened. She fell asleep with Mac's arms around her, and his slow breathing lulling her the way a gentle night breeze rocks a boat at anchor. She let herself feel sheltered, secure, serene, and drifted into a dreamless sleep.

That feeling of serenity didn't quite survive the night. She woke early, and lay there thinking things over for an hour before Mac even stirred.

Well, partly she was thinking things over. Partly she was just watching him, feeling the familiar grab of desire in her belly that overtook her whenever she was this near to him. The tangle of his unruly hair was driving her wild. The gentle curve of his closed eyelids was unbearably seductive. That damned little smile that tilted his lips even in a deep sleep made her want to fling caution to the winds and do crazy, un-Hilary-like things.

She'd already done them, and more, last night. This morning, she decided reluctantly, was for looking at the situation in a more realistic light. She finally gave up her innocent ogling and the not-so-innocent pleasure it filled her with, and slid out from under the sheet Mac had pulled over both of them sometime in the night.

She helped herself to his shower, and emerged freshly scrubbed and dressed to find him up and making coffee in the kitchen. The coffee, or something else, seemed to be having an exhilarating effect on his spirits. He was grinning widely.

"Thought you'd abandoned me," he told her.

"Don't worry. That's not my style." She tied the belt of her dress, and felt a little antsy about what she had to say next.

He beat her to the draw. "How about this as a plan for the rest of the day?" he was saying. "My parents are having sort of a garden party at their summer place up in the Gatineaus. I promised I'd put in an appearance if I got back in time, because there's someone there I need to meet. Place'll be crawling with diplomats and dignitaries, I'm afraid, but the location is beautiful—on one of the quietest, clearest lakes you've ever seen—and my mother's a great cook."

He poured water into his coffee filter with a flamboyant gesture. Hilary waited silently, feeling her cautious optimism evaporating like the steam that rose above the coffeepot.

"I promise to keep the business part of the thing to a minimum, and then we can just enjoy the lake and the sunshine," he went on. "It would be a crime to waste such a nice day, right?"

"Wrong." She hated to say it, but there was no use pretending she could go along with this. "I can't do it, Mac."

"Why not? Good food, boats, hardly any mosquitoes—what's to object to?"

"Try this on for size—a refrigerator that's nearly as empty as yours, two sons who have to be picked up at the train station and approximately four tons of laundry that needs to be done to get ready for the first week of school."

"Oh." He had the grace to look disconcerted. "Common sense slams broadside into moonshine again, eh?"

"I'm afraid so." She kept her voice steady, not wanting to betray how close she'd been to asking him to come and keep her company through the mundane details of her day. She'd had a small, lost hope that it might appeal to him.

"I'm sorry, Hilary." He paused in making the coffee. "I'd get out of this party if I could, but the guy I'm supposed to meet is someone who might be my next boss, depending on where I get posted. It's sort of important for me to see him."

"Of course, I understand." Why was she saying *Of course, I understand* when her whole brain was screaming with *I knew this would happen?*

Because she didn't want to parade her private hurts in front of him, that was why. She closed down her deepest feelings as they drank a noncommittal cup of coffee together, and then she left, after giving him a vague and equally noncommittal answer to his question about when he could see her again.

Getting home to her comfortable, familiar house was both a relief and a terrible wrench. She threw herself into the domestic joys of sorting laundry and making lists, trying as hard as she knew how to still the fierce demons of longing and hope that still roiled around inside her.

Four loads of dirty clothes were an astonishingly welcome distraction. Laundry, in her present state of mind, was a far simpler thing to cope with than love.

Tuesday started and ended in an uproar. Getting the boys reacclimatized to the idea of early rising was always a chore. Hilary made breakfast, packed lunches, talked Todd out of wearing an outfit consisting of screaming green Spandex biking shorts and a yowling pink T-shirt he'd won at the midway in Toronto this weekend, and realized, when she listened to Andrew making veiled but obviously reverent remarks about one of the girls in his grade, that romance had been added to the three R's in his school life. The thought made her feel old.

Impossible as it seemed, the boys were nearly fifteen. She'd only been eighteen when they were born. *Keep your heads on straight, guys,* she exhorted them silently as she watched them charge down the steps on their way to school. *Don't jump into adulthood, like I did.*

Her own head was anything but straight as she walked along Wellington Street to open her shop just before ten. She was thinking hard about Mac, about his career and his far-flung adventurous spirit and the way her pulse raced whenever he looked at her with that tilted grin.

She was thinking, too, about the fact that when he'd disappeared for two weeks, it had never even occurred to him to have someone else come in and watch his shop. She was glad he'd taken the extra two minutes to write a note sending his customers over to *Fortissimo,* but a part of her was annoyed with him for being so cavalier.

Hilary Gardiner, you are a piece of work, she told herself as she neared her own store. You're just as irked by his sloppy business practices as you are with the fact that he's there in the first place. That's not normal, woman.

Neither was the thought of a life without Mac, at this point. She cast her mind back over the summer they'd shared, the crazy picnics, with whole armies of little hot sauce bottles dotting Mac's checkered picnic blanket, the idyllic day of kite flying, the blissful, childlike, utter freedom she felt when she was with him.

Take that away, and she knew she'd age ten years in a minute. She wanted her swashbuckling lover, and all the things he made her feel.

Did she want him enough to give up the things she had? At the moment, *Fortissimo,* with its mounting debts and dismal future, didn't seem like much of a reason to throw away a future with the man she loved. And Todd and Andrew were young, and resilient. Maybe they would take to a change of scenery better than she'd been imagining up until now.

Her mind was casting around among all these possibilities as she reached the store, and it took a moment to realize that Santa Claus had been there during the night.

Evidently he'd used an employee of Canada Post as his courier. But he'd certainly sent her some goodies, because there was a big canvas bag sitting on her doorstep, and it seemed to be filled to the brim.

She unlocked the door and hauled the bag inside. She pulled out a handful of letters, and read the first one. It was from a woman in Manitoba, who said she'd read about *Fortissimo* in a well-known women's magazine. She thought hot sauces sounded like a great gift idea. Would *Fortissimo* please send her its catalog?

"We don't have a catalog," Hilary said out loud to the empty store.

The next three letters said the same thing. Hilary stared at the bulging bag, and slowly came alive to the realization that it contained hundreds and hundreds of potential customers. She read two more letters, her fingers shaking slightly now, and then she reached for the phone and called Karen.

"Can you come over here?" she said. "We're snowed under."

"Hilary, it's only September. Too early for snow."

Hilary told her the good news. Karen whooped, and promised to be over in two minutes with her trusty letter opener.

It took her longer than two minutes, because she'd wisely stopped to pick up a copy of the magazine the letters had referred to. The two women laughed in delight over the short but eye-catching spread devoted to *Fortissimo.* The article managed to imply that hot food was *the* new trend in dining, and that sauces from the Ottawa store would make great Christmas gifts.

"This is beyond wonderful," Karen pronounced. "We're talking major circulation here, Hilary. I have a feeling this is going to be your big break."

"*Our* big break." Hilary made the correction automatically as she dug into the bag for more letters. "I can't wait to tell the boys!"

"*And* the bank."

"I'd honestly forgotten all about talking to that writer," Hilary confessed. "It was ages ago, long before the store opened. And she didn't seem all that interested. I had a feeling nothing would come of it."

"That'll teach you to trust your feelings," Karen crowed. "There's only one thing."

"What?"

"We don't have a catalog to send all these nice people."

"I know. When I talked to that woman I was thinking in vague terms of expanding into mail order some bright day way off in the future."

"It looks like the bright day just arrived without warning," Karen said. "How soon can we get a catalog together?"

"Sooner than you'd think." Hilary's mind was racing, her spirits buoyed by this sudden good luck. "Gift baskets, Karen. We'll have to advertise gift baskets for Christmas. I bet they'll sell like crazy. Remember that guy from school who was going to start a graphic design shop? Can you call him and see if he's available? I'll start writing copy, and we can go to the post office this afternoon to see about bulk mail."

There weren't many customers during the day—they'd all headed back to Mac's for Ste. Helenean firepower, she figured—but for the first time it didn't bother her. She was up to her eyelids in plans, and she didn't even realize it was getting near closing time until a small army of teenage boys invaded the shop, led by Todd and Andrew.

"This is Daniel and Curtis," Todd said, waving to his friends. "You know Simon and Jim and Dylan. My mom," he added to the boys.

Hilary smiled at them all. "Hi, guys," she said. "Come to check out the hot stuff?"

Andrew was already collecting the free-sample jars and bottles she kept in a small refrigerator behind the counter. "They *think* they're tough," he said. "We told them we'd see about that."

There was a chorus of bravado from the five boys. Hilary helped Todd and Andrew set up a chili-laced obstacle course for their friends to try, starting with the mild burn of a red barbecue sauce and ending, for the very brave, with a fiery Jamaican concoction that made her own eyes sting as soon as she took the lid off.

They were all determined to show no pain. Hilary smiled at the array of reddened ears, watering eyes and manfully suppressed yelps as they worked their way through the sample jars. In between offering encouragement and glasses of water, she told Todd and Andrew about the mountain of mail they'd gotten that day.

"All *right*," Todd cheered. "Fame and fortune, here we come."

"I'd settle for solvency," Hilary said.

"You've gotta think big, Mom. This is the big one for *Fortissimo*. I have a feeling. Hey, Dylan, man, go easy on that one. It's a killer."

Dylan, encouraged by the fact that he'd survived the second hottest sauce, and unversed in the ways of the Scotch bonnet pepper, was spooning a taste of Hilary's most potent product. He put it in his mouth, and started to grin triumphantly. The grin turned to astonishment, then to regret, then to horror. A moment later he was writhing histrionically against the wall and there was a chorus of sympathetic laughter all around him.

Hilary joined in. And a moment later, she became aware that another laugh had joined in, too. A deeper sound, ringing and free.

Mac. She hadn't heard him come into the shop. She turned to see him standing at the door, hands on his hips, his mouth curved into a smile and his eyes dancing wickedly. Beyond him, at the curb, she could see his disreputable motorcycle.

"Should I call the fire department?" he asked.

"Either that or Actor's Equity," she replied, still laughing. "I haven't seen this good a death scene since Olivier's *Richard III.*"

Dylan was calling weakly for water. Todd administered it, and then caught sight of Mac.

"Hey, Mac," he called. "Show these guys how it's done, okay?"

Mac sauntered up to the array of hot sauces and unerringly picked up the one that had nearly finished off Dylan. The circle of boys parted respectfully, and Hilary heard quiet *oohs* and *aahs* as he calmly ate a spoonful of the scorching stuff.

"Years of practice, guys," he said solemnly. "Hard work and sacrifice. That's what it takes."

They treated him to an appreciative round of applause.

"And now, if you don't mind, I'd like to talk to this lady alone," he added, and took Hilary's elbow. His still-awed audience moved aside to let him steer Hilary out the front door.

Behind her, she could hear fragments of conversation.

"That your mother's boyfriend?" one of the kids was asking.

At the tag end of Todd's answer she heard the words "...has his own airplane...used to fly it around the Caribbean."

She frowned. The day had been such a tornado that she'd barely drawn breath since ten o'clock. She wanted time to think, but Mac was obviously not going to give it to her.

What was behind that dancing glee in his hazel eyes? She looked hard at him, and said, "I didn't know you were a pilot."

"Among other things." He waved the question away. "Listen, Hilary, I need to talk to you. Have dinner with me this evening."

She shook her head. "Sorry, Mac. The boys and I have a date. I always take them out for pizza after the first day of school. It started out as a bribe, but now it's a family tradition. You can join us if you like."

Was that wise? She wasn't sure. All she knew was that she wanted to be with him.

He was declining her offer with what looked like regret. "What I need to talk about can't be said in front of the boys," he said firmly. "Come and have a drink with me, then. Before dinner."

"I have to close up the store."

"How long will that take?"

"Well..." She looked inside, where the seven hulking teenagers were screwing the lids back on the lethal jars of sauce. "Not long, I guess. I just have to take the deposit to the bank."

"Let Todd and Andrew do that. I really have to talk to you, Hilary. And I'm going away again later tonight, so I don't have a lot of time."

Her heart clenched in apprehension. "Going away...to Ste. Helene?"

He nodded, but that devil's grin was still in his eyes. "It's no fluke this time," he said. "But I have to talk to you first."

She hesitated for a long moment. She knew what was making her feel so upside-down: in the past eight hours, the prospects for her financial future had turned a hundred and eighty degrees. She was becoming more anchored, more rooted to home.

She looked at Mac, at his dancing eyes and easy, long-legged stance. He was feeling the deck of a ship rolling underneath him again, she thought. She could see it in his smile. And she was feeling more earthbound than ever.

Still, she wanted to know what he had to say to her. She nodded finally, and pushed open *Fortissimo*'s door to ask Todd and Andrew if they would take the deposit to the bank and lock up for her.

"We'll all do it," Andrew promised. "You got an armed guard, Mom."

"Armed with this," said Dylan, who seemed to have recovered. He waved a bottle of Scotch bonnet sauce in the air.

"Don't forget about our pizza, Mom," Todd added. "You want to come, Mac?"

"Sorry, guys. Maybe next time."

"Boy, do we have stuff to celebrate tonight," Todd said. "Wait'll you hear, Mom. Mr. Devon, the principal, liked that story Andrew wrote last spring so much, he said he wants Andrew to adapt it and stage it for the school play this year. Isn't that cool?"

There was a buzz of approval from the boys. Hilary could hear Mac's deep voice among the others, approving, congratulating, being accepted as one of them. *Almost as if he belonged.*

"That's great, honey," she said automatically, and prayed they wouldn't hear the quiver in her voice.

Fifteen minutes ago she'd been as lighthearted as her own sons, laughing with them at everything and nothing. Now she felt the familiar bands of caution and anxiety start to tighten around her heart again. Her life, her sons' lives, were so rooted in this city, and the circle of friends they had here.

The thought of Mac zipping off to Ste. Helene again later tonight made her feel he was an attractive alien who'd just happened to stray by en route to another galaxy. He *didn't* belong here, and there was no getting around that.

Unless, by some miracle, the things he was so eager to say to her could provide a way around all that. Having had more than her share of miracles this summer, Hilary wasn't about to write off the possibility. She grabbed her handbag, told the boys she'd meet them at home in an hour, and allowed herself to be hoisted onto the back of Mac's big purple bike as though she, and not the cheering crowd at the door of her shop, were the one barely into her teens.

They ended up at Domingo's. "You seem to have a homing instinct about this place," Hilary said, as they went inside.

"It's a fatal weakness for the food," Mac said. He squired her to a corner table with a jauntiness that she found a little unnerving. He was usually confident and cocky, it was true. But what was behind this sudden spring in his step, and the glint in his eye that just wouldn't quit?

She had to know. "I have to be home by six, Mac," she pointed out. "What's on your mind?"

"First of all, this." He'd pulled her chair out for her, and now, as she sat down, he leaned over and kissed the place where her neck sloped into her collarbone. She felt her blood rush to the spot, and then race madly into every corner of her being, carrying the good news that the magic of his touch hadn't lost any of its potency since she'd seen him yesterday.

"And I want you to know," he added, lips still grazing her neck as though he had plans to seduce her right then and there, "that I get extra chocolate-covered brownie points for not kissing you in front of that crowd in your store."

"You impressed them enough as it was." She couldn't get the words out calmly. "Mac, please. What did you want to tell me?"

He must have heard the plea in her voice, because he gave her one more gentle kiss and seated himself opposite her. "I've never done this before," he said, "so I'll keep it short and simple. I want to talk about getting married."

Mac saw the astonishment on her face, and he couldn't help laughing. The laughter was an outlet for everything he was feeling, the relief at having solved their problems, his ridiculous pride in Hilary's dark-haired beauty and warm, giving spirit, his love for her.

He expected her to laugh with him. When she didn't, he hurried to explain, "About us getting married, I mean. I know this seems sudden, but—well, hell." He had to laugh again. "I get my ideas like lightning flashes, Hilary. This one struck me the moment I got out of bed. Whether you noticed it or not, you weren't in my bed this morning."

"I noticed it." Surely she'd felt the jolt as much as he had, the wrenching sense of loss at waking up and not being together. His lightning flash had followed hard on that feeling of loss.

"Well, I don't want that to happen again, lady. I want to be with you, whenever and wherever possible. I want to look into those blue eyes every morning of my life. I don't want us to be apart, not anymore, Hilary."

He'd ordered two beers when they'd arrived. The waiter brought them to the table now, but neither of them drank. Mac was feeling so effervescent already that he had no need of alcohol, but Hilary's stillness and silence were something he hadn't expected. He could have sworn a spasm of pain crossed her face, leaving a troubled shadow in those multihued blue eyes.

"Where?" she said.

The single word brought him up short. "Anywhere," he said. "Everywhere. Wherever we happen to be."

"Wherever *you* happen to be, you mean." Her voice was small and definitely not happy.

Mac leaned his elbows on the table, as if he could warm her with his closeness. "My job calls for a lot of traveling," he said, aware that that was the understatement of the evening. He leaned a little closer, and delivered the news that he was sure would crack that serious veneer on her face. "But here's the good news, Hilary. Remember the guy I had to meet yesterday?"

She nodded, studying him, somber and watchful.

"He's going to be my new boss, in London. England," he added.

"I've heard of it."

This wasn't going the way he'd envisioned. He'd imagined Hilary bursting with pleasure and relief, seeing immediately the new possibilities that lay before them. Instead, she'd folded her hands delicately on the tabletop and was giving him a considering stare that made him feel he'd just breached some rule he hadn't even been aware of.

"Hilary, it's the answer to all those problems we've been talking about. I'll be posted there for a while, definitely until the boys are ready for university. And London has some of the best schools in the English-speaking world. There won't be any problem on that front."

Her stare intensified. He almost thought he saw the sheen of tears behind it. He frowned. "And it's a big city, with cosmopolitan tastes. Transfer *Fortissimo* there, and you'll be an instant hit. I feel it in my bones."

He had an uneasy feeling he wasn't the only one whose bones were telling him things. Her next words proved it.

"My life is here."

She spoke so softly he had to lean even farther forward to catch what she'd said.

He made his voice as persuasive as he knew how. She'd been jolted hard in her life, jarred by disillusionment and solitary hard work. It was time to make her believe he wouldn't let her down, couldn't, in fact. He couldn't imagine a life without her, and that was the simple truth.

"Your life *has* been here," he said. "I accept that. But you're not looking at what it could be. There's an adventurous spirit lurking behind those eyes of yours, Hilary. I've seen it. You can try to hide it, but I know it's there."

Right now the only thing lurking in her eyes was pain, raw and unadulterated. Mac felt a sudden lurch of fear. He didn't count on success before it happened, as he'd told Hilary already. But he didn't dwell on failure overmuch, either. The idea that she might refuse to marry him struck him with the force of a sailboat's boom swinging around too fast and out of control.

"We can't leave, Mac," she said. "You heard what Todd said. Andrew's supposed to write the school play this year."

He just stared at her. Then he laughed. This laugh wasn't quite as full of confidence as the previous one had been.

"Are you telling me you won't marry me and come to London because Andrew has to write the school play?" he demanded. She must be joking with him. She had to be.

Her eyes told him she wasn't. "It's not just the play," she said. "It's the school. They love it there. I used to have to take them out for pizza because otherwise they dreaded the first day of school. Now we go out to celebrate, because they enjoy it so much. They have good friends, friends they've known almost all their lives."

The sudden catch in her voice made Mac's own throat tight. She was trying to tell him *no*. His gut fought against it, and his hands. They balled into fists on the tabletop.

"And my store—" She gulped in some air, and went on more calmly. "I had a lightning bolt of my own today," she said. "We got written up in a major women's magazine, and all of a sudden I've got mail orders coming out of the cracks in the wall. It looks like *Fortissimo* is going to be a success whether or not you stick around, Mac."

"But Hilary, that's great!" His enthusiasm was honest and heartfelt. "I knew you could do it."

"You're missing the point." There was an edge of desperation to what she was saying. "I can't leave now. Now, of all times."

"But a mail-order business is the most portable kind in the world. You can operate it from anywhere."

"I don't want to operate it from anywhere. I want to operate it from here." The stubborn set of her eyebrows made him very, very nervous. "I want to see this store succeed— this particular one, that I've put so much work into. I want to raise my sons among their friends, not uproot them just when they're starting to grow up and feel some confidence about the world. I know all about being uprooted, Mac, and it's not something I choose to do to Todd and Andrew."

"I spent my childhood being 'uprooted,' as you call it," he told her. "I loved it. I thought it was a great adventure."

"And what did you plan to be when you grew up?" she demanded.

He felt sort of silly confessing his childhood ambition, but what the hell... "A pirate," he said, and grinned sheepishly. "Promise you won't tell."

The look of longing and unhappiness that invaded her face was something he didn't think he'd ever forget. What had caused that sudden agony of loss in her eyes?

"Todd wants to be an architect," she said. The prosaic words were at odds with the roughness of tears in her voice. "Andrew wants to go to journalism school. Those aren't great adventures, Mac. My boys are homebodies. Just like their mother."

She started to get out of her chair. Mac seized hold of her wrists, and tugged her back down.

"Are you telling me you don't want to marry me?" he said bluntly. God, this couldn't be the end of it! There had to be somewhere to go from here.

"No." For a moment he wasn't sure what she meant. Then she explained, her eyes wide and haunted and a hundred different shades of mysterious blue. "I want to marry you more than I can tell you. I want to be with you all the time, more than I can imagine. But I can't dig up all my roots to do it. Not even for you."

This time she got away from him. Mac scowled and flung some money on the table to pay for the two beers they hadn't even touched. He caught up with her at the door, having punctuated his progress through the small, dark restaurant with some of the more colorful phrases he'd picked up in his sojourn in the Caribbean.

He ignored the raised eyebrows of the staff as he stormed out of the place. Catching up with Hilary was all that mattered.

"Are you planning to walk home?" he demanded.

"No. Cab." She didn't seem to want to trust her voice. Good. Maybe that meant there was still room for negotiation, for hope.

"Don't be crazy. I'll drive you."

She shook her head. Her shining black hair swayed like a gentle breeze. How could anyone so lovely, so gentle, so humorous, so filled with barely veiled passion that it stirred him even while he wanted to wring her neck—how could one woman be breaking his heart like this?

"I mean it, Hilary. It's rush hour. You'll wait forever for a cab. Get on the bike."

"I can't." Her voice was small again.

"Why not, for God's sake?"

His fears were making him harsh with her. He knew it, but he couldn't stop himself. She had no right to shake him like this. No woman ever had. No woman had ever made him want to get married, to spend the rest of his days making love to her. He'd fallen for Hilary Gardiner like a tumbling house of cards, and now she was turning him down.

He couldn't quite catch her words. A truck roared by, masking them. But he caught the jist of it, something about being too close, and too difficult.

Maybe physical closeness was the only way out of this. It had already proved to her more than once that what they felt for each other was worth acting on. He crossed his fingers for luck, rolled his eyes for show and insisted—positively insisted, with a high-handedness he'd found came in handy in all kinds of sticky situations—that he was going to give her a lift home. Then he helped her onto the Triumph and gunned the thing to life.

It was perhaps the longest motorcycle ride Mac could remember taking, including the time he'd driven solo from Montreal to Washington, D.C., with barely time to stop for gas. He'd been in serious pain when he'd finally stopped, but it had been nothing compared with this.

Hilary clung to him like a vine, circling him with her arms as though she never wanted to let him go. And maybe she didn't. She'd just admitted that much to him. He could feel her soft curves molded to him, fitting him so perfectly that in spite of his frustration and the rush-hour traffic, he felt the undeniable stirring of desire.

Great. Here, on a motorcycle, with desperate bureaucrats all still driving like they hadn't figured out it wasn't the long weekend anymore. Concentrating was fiendishly hard.

He felt Hilary burrow a little more deeply into his shoulder, and he couldn't repress a moan. He should pull over, take her in his arms, demand that she not turn her back on their love.

Here, on Wellington Street? Even if there were anywhere to stop, the busy street, with its stores and pedestrians and traffic lights, was about the least romantic location Mac could have picked. He should have driven off with her, carried her with him over the river to the park, laid her down among the trees and made her eyes brim over with longing the way they had only two days ago.

Well, he was stuck with Wellington Street for now. He'd pull into her driveway and turn around on the Triumph's seat and tell her—well, he'd figure out what to tell her once he got the chance to soften whatever words he chose with a kiss. Or more than one.

He could almost taste her lips, and the sweet, honeyed coolness of her mouth. Thank God they were at her street by now. He turned off the busy strip and into her quiet neighborhood. The sensation of having Hilary glued to him like this, while the unruly old motorcycle roared and vibrated between his legs, was making his head swim and his fingers curl with remembered pleasure.

She must be feeling the same things herself. She held on to him so tightly, almost as if she were seeing him for the first time in ages.

Or as if she were saying goodbye. The thought struck him with chilling clarity. He thundered into her driveway, killed the engine and vaulted off the bike. The silence was suddenly loud, and Hilary's calmness unnerving.

She slid off the other side of the seat with a decisiveness he didn't like. "Hilary, wait," he said. "We haven't finished this."

"*I've* finished."

Mac swallowed past a gigantic lump in his throat. His gut lurched, wild with desire and the fear of losing her.

"It can't work, Mac. I'm sorry. Goodbye."

Just like that. With those few quiet, corny, hackneyed—hell, clichéd—words, she was gone. Up the stairs, into the house. And he knew with a dead certainty that she wasn't going to come out again.

"Well, I'll be damned."

He said the words out loud to a rhododendron bush, which, as bushes will, offered little or no helpful advice. The neat chintz curtains on her living room window were similarly uncommunicative. Mac swatted a glossy green leaf with sudden anger, and climbed back onto his bike.

It wasn't until he was stopped at a traffic light that he realized the back of his shirt was damp. He reached a hand over his shoulder, and felt a small patch of moisture that hadn't been there when he and Hilary had left the restaurant.

The thought of her sitting back there, clinging to him, crying, saying goodbye, threatened to choke him. He gunned the motorcycle ferociously, frightening several respectable-looking citizens around him. When the light changed, he took off as if, with enough velocity, careers and friends and beautiful blue-eyed women and maybe even gravity itself could be overcome.

Ten

Thank God for *Fortissimo*. The store kept Hilary up late and woke her early in the morning. It had her running from the graphic designer to the post office, from wicker wholesalers to gift-wrap outlets. It gave her hands and feet and brain a hundred things to do, and a dozen places to go.

It gave her something to do on the outside while her heart, on the inside, was grieving about Mac.

She'd done the right thing. She was almost sure of that. The tiny part of her that wasn't absolutely convinced, even now, kept whispering that she'd turned her back on the one man who'd ever made her feel whole and alive and free. Those thoughts gnawed at her in the few moments she *didn't* manage to fill up with *Fortissimo*-related business.

Mostly, though, she kept busy. On Friday night, four days after Mac had roared out of her driveway on that smoke-belching, oil-leaking behemoth of his, she was busy typing addresses into her computer's data base, generating a mailing list that would bring her lots and lots of customers who would continue to keep her busy so that she could continue not dwelling on Mac. The boys were allegedly in the room next to her small basement office, doing their homework.

That is, they were definitely in the next room, but only allegedly doing homework. She could hear the muted sound of the television, and she was debating whether to go in there and check whether the homework was, in fact, done.

She took a brief break from typing addresses. It was astonishing how even a tiny space of time like this could fill up instantly with thoughts of Mac, with longing for him and feeling a howling gale of loneliness inside when she realized that what they'd had together was over.

Anything was better than letting herself drown in those thoughts again. She'd been over and over them at 3:00 a.m. every night since he'd left, and it didn't make the pain any easier to take. Sighing, Hilary pushed herself back from her makeshift desk, and went into the next room.

She arrived just as Todd was calling her. "Hey, Mom," he said. "Is this ever cool! Come and watch."

She went in expecting some new music video of the sort Todd and Andrew liked and she never could understand— the kind with lots of dry ice and tight clothes and expressions that ranged from pained to bored. What she got was a close-up of Mac's face, grinning at the camera.

There was a blue, blue ocean behind him. She could see him squinting a little against the tropical brightness of the sun. Damn it, there was even a breeze lifting his curls, so that they glinted gold in the sunlight. He looked the way he had in her dreams: rakish and too good-looking to be true, with that subtle hint of seriousness beneath the curve of his smile.

He must be on a boat somewhere. The camera kept tilting, and the horizon, behind Mac's smiling face, wouldn't hold still. It was the way she'd always pictured him, on the high seas, raffish, unencumbered, standing there with his knees slightly bent to move with the ocean's sway.

She knew exactly how the muscles of his thighs would look, tight against the old jeans he almost always wore. She knew how his dark brown hair would feel, warmed by the sun and lifted by the wind's caress.

It was all she could do to suppress a moan of mingled loss and desire. He looked so utterly cavalier, so perfect for the renegade part he'd chosen to play. When her blood stopped humming in her ears, she finally tuned in to what he was doing on her television screen.

"They said he rescued some guy off Ste. Helene," Andrew filled in for her. "They got shot at or something, and he had to try for an emergency landing on this island that's only about half a mile long."

Dear God, what next? She could imagine him doing it, too.

One of the reporters—there was obviously a horde of them—was asking Mac how he'd gotten to his friend in the first place. Mac just grinned at the question.

"With a lot of help, and a lot of luck," was his answer. "I can't claim all the credit for this, by any means."

"But Mr. MacDougall, it *was* your plane that took Mr. Dubose off the island, was it not?"

The grin faded a bit. "*Was,* as in past tense," he said. "I can't say I'd want to make that approach again in this lifetime. We were damn lucky we came out of it alive."

The shot changed. Now the camera was panning over the rocky shore of a tiny island, a mass of sharp black rock against that impossibly blue sea. In the curling foam at the base of one long sloping hillside, there was a small airplane, or what had been a small airplane. Hilary caught her breath.

"He tried to land on *that?*" she said out loud.

"They said the security forces hit his rudder, and there was no way he could keep flying. It was either the island, or crash into the water," Todd said.

Hilary was speechless.

The deep voice of the television anchorman took over. "Whether MacDougall's daring rescue will have international repercussions is not yet known. Ste. Helenean government personnel have declined to issue a statement saying why MacDougall's plane was fired on. Previous communiqués have referred to Henry Dubose as 'a dangerous subversive,' a charge denied by the Ste. Helenean community in Canada. Dubose will be joining his wife, Sarah, in Ottawa, and applying for political asylum."

The camera returned to the swaying boat and Mac's smiling face. The shot showed him standing next to a tall, thin black man with a short beard speckled in gray. He was smiling, too, but tiredly, as though he wasn't quite sure how he'd gotten there.

Hilary watched Mac reach over and touch the other man's shoulder reassuringly. She straightened her own shoulders, as if she felt that familiar touch. Then the two men raised their clasped hands in the air, a victory salute for the benefit of the cameramen, and the story was over.

"Wow." There was awe in Todd's voice. "They said he landed on Ste. Helene at night, without any lights, and picked this guy up. Can you believe it, Mom?"

"I can believe it." Of course she could believe it. This was how Mac lived his life, how he'd chosen to be. She didn't like it a whole lot, but she had no trouble believing it.

"I also believe it's nearly time for bed," she went on, before she could get drawn into any further talk about Mac's crazy adventure. "Homework all done?"

"Aw, Mom." Todd sounded aggrieved. "You haven't had to bug us about homework for years."

"What do you want for lunch tomorrow?" she asked them, as the three of them headed upstairs.

She could feel their surprised stares through her shoulder blades. "You never ask us what we want for lunch," Andrew pointed out.

"Well, tonight I'm asking. Tuna fish okay? Or would you rather have salmon?"

She paused in the kitchen, and saw them exchanging a glance. "Tuna's fine," Andrew said.

"Good. Can you come by the store and give me a hand unpacking some stuff tomorrow after school?" She knew she was running on at the mouth, but she couldn't help it. Anything was better than having the conversation turn to Mac.

"We already said we would." Todd sounded puzzled, but Andrew, always a little more sensitive, seemed to have figured out what was really going on. He paused on his way upstairs, looming over Hilary as he stood on the first step.

"It's okay, Mom," he said, in that deep voice she couldn't quite get used to. "We'll all survive."

He was telling her, in that understated way he had, that the end of her relationship with Mac was no secret to the boys. Hilary felt her eyes swim with unexpected tears. They were so dear, these two, and just as supportive of her as she'd ever been of them.

She loved Andrew's careful, oblique way of phrasing things. He wasn't going to come right out and say anything baldly. But he was telling her clearly that whatever she chose to do, he and his brother would understand.

There was something so homey about her little family, something so *right*. Guns and political prisoners and midnight landings without lights on deserted tropical islands had no place here. They belonged on the television, not in her life.

As she hugged her sons good-night, still battling the stubborn tears that wouldn't quite leave, she felt a new and painful certainty that she really had done the right thing in refusing to consider Mac's proposal of marriage. What she had here was something she didn't ever want to give up.

"Oh, Mac," she whispered, leaning on the banister when the boys were gone. "Why couldn't you have wanted this, too?"

She had an unexpected visitor in the store the next day.

She was unloading some boxes from her car when a cab pulled into the empty parking space behind her. To Hilary's surprise, the driver got out and lifted a wooden crate out of the cab's trunk, and headed toward *Fortissimo*'s door with it.

"Where you want this, lady?" he called over his shoulder.

Hilary put down the cardboard box she was holding. "I think you've got the wrong address," she said. "I didn't order any deliveries by cab."

"No, but I did." Hilary turned to see a white-haired woman getting out of the cab's back seat. "Are you Hilary?"

"Yes, but—"

She was sure she'd never seen the woman before. But something was nagging at her as she took in the details of the very pleasantly wrinkled face, the subdued but obviously well-made brown jacket and skirt, and the twinkle in the eye. Most of all, the twinkle in the eye.

"Then why don't you show this nice gentleman where he can put these crates, and I'll explain."

The authoritative air, too, had something familiar about it. Hilary propped the shop door open, and watched the cabdriver trek in with three heavy wooden crates. All of them had "Ste. Helene" lettered on their sides.

"Thank you," the older woman said graciously. She asked the driver to wait a few minutes, and then accompanied Hilary inside. "You must be wondering what's going on," she said. Her manner was one Hilary could have grown to like: pleasant, diplomatic, yet straightforward. Two things occurred to her, one being that of course a diplomat's wife would have to learn to be a diplomat herself.

The other was that she wasn't going to get a chance to grow to like Mac's mother. This was part of an ending, not a new beginning.

"I think I know part of what's going on," she said, leaning on the counter. "You're Mrs. MacDougall, aren't you?"

The woman twinkled at her. "What gave me away? The crates?"

"Partly." *Those hazel eyes, mostly.*

"Well, people always say Mac looks like his father, but maybe he gets something from me, too. Hilary, I hope I'm doing the right thing in following my son's instructions. When he called, I wasn't sure what to think."

That combined charm and sense of purpose were obviously something else Mac had come by honestly. "When did he call?" Hilary forced herself to ask casually.

"Saturday, two days after that escapade of his on Ste. Helene. He said he was held up with red tape, but he wanted to make sure all his leftover stock of food from Ste. Helene came to you. When I asked him if the two of you had a business arrangement, he got all vague on me." The look in her hazel eyes was anything but vague.

She hadn't asked a direct question, but Hilary knew one was implied. "We had another sort of arrangement," she said slowly. "But it didn't work out."

Mac's mother nodded briskly. "Well, I've learned from years of experience that I'll get nowhere by trying to interfere in Mac's life. He keeps his own counsel, and always has." She straightened the front of her expensive tweed jacket and added, "I'll be out of your way, now that I've done what I said I would. Perhaps I'll see you again, Hilary. I gather Mac's closing up that place of his now that he's gotten his friend off the island."

"He said he would likely do that." Hilary couldn't believe how normal and calm her voice sounded. Inside she felt ripped apart, wanting to be free of all her complicated longings for Mac, but also hating to cut this one last tie with him.

"Well, he's leaving me stranded, because I'm actually starting to acquire a taste for hot food, after all these years. Maybe I'll just have to come in and buy some from you, once Mac's gone."

Did she have any idea what was going on inside Hilary? From something in the older woman's face, Hilary thought maybe she did. The notion made her bold enough to ask a direct question, and foolhardy enough not to care that her voice shook when she asked it.

"Mrs. MacDougall, you've lived all over the world, haven't you?"

Mac's mother gave her a shrewd look. "Sometimes I feel I've seen nearly every corner of it," she replied.

Hilary's hands were tightly curled into fists in her skirt pocket. "Would you say it gave you a chance to have a good family life?" she asked.

She could see the older woman giving the question careful consideration. Hilary found herself holding her breath, as though a positive answer, even at this late date, might be enough to give her some hope that she and Mac might still work things out.

But the answer wasn't positive. Finally Mrs. Mac-Dougall shook her white head and said gently, "I have to say that the life was much better for my husband than it was for me. It isn't easy, you know, adjusting oneself to every new posting." She gave a rueful laugh. "Sometimes I felt we'd been beamed onto a different planet every time we had to shift from one place to another. Even Ottawa took some getting used to, when we finally came back here. You can feel terribly isolated, you know, living that kind of life. It makes putting down roots really very difficult."

Hilary couldn't think of an answer. She was lost in her own thoughts when Mac's mother added, "I hope I haven't discouraged you, my dear."

The kindness in the older woman's voice made Hilary's stiff upper lip quiver. "No," she said, with a desperate kind of honesty. "You haven't discouraged me at all. You've just confirmed what I was thinking all along."

And now that it was confirmed, there was nothing more for her to do than try to accept the fact that Mac's life was simply not for her, and concentrate on getting on with the life she'd chosen. She had to do it, even though half the laughter and all the spice seemed to have gone out of her world when her pirate lover had sailed away with her heart.

The reception was hot and noisy. Usually Mac liked heat and didn't mind noise. Usually he was thrilled when a formal reception started to turn itself into a plain old party, as this one was beginning to do. Tonight he couldn't wait to escape.

Escaping was difficult, because he was the guest of honor. His friends from Ste. Helene, and their friends, and practically everyone they'd ever met, it seemed, were all gathered at Domingo's to celebrate Mac's rescue and Henry's reunion with his compatriots and his wife. It was a big, festive, family kind of gathering. And it was driving Mac up the wall.

He told himself it was just because he was supposed to leave for London in a week, and he was feeling rushed. There were too many things to do: close up his shop in the market, be debriefed on the Caribbean and filled in on the United Kingdom, spend some time with his parents. For some reason his mother had suddenly been getting all solicitous about him, asking him whether he was really sure this posting in England was a good idea.

"Sure it's a good idea," he'd told her. "It's a step up the ladder for me—a big step. And anyway, it's External's idea, so even if I didn't like it, I'd still be going."

He'd been that way with everyone since he'd come home from Ste. Helene: blunt, choppy and not terribly uncommunicative. Because what he hadn't told anyone, not Henry, not Sarah, not his mother, was that he felt as though someone had sucked all the juice out of his life while he'd been on Ste. Helene.

He'd left in a fine blaze of anger about Hilary and the way she'd turned him down. *Fine,* he told himself. If things weren't going to work out, it was better to find out now than halfway around the world when she'd already pulled up her stakes and tied her life to his. It was definitely better this way.

Except that even in the throes of a rescue attempt that had had more blood-racing, heart-pounding near misses than anything he'd ever attempted before, all he could think about was Hilary.

He'd felt anger, all right, when those damned trigger-happy soldiers had started firing off rounds of antiaircraft fire at him, but it had been Hilary he was angry at. And even in those awful moments when he'd realized there was no way to avoid crashing his plane, when he'd watched the black rocks getting closer and closer and grabbed desperately for what little control he still had over the craft—even then, the thought uppermost in his mind was that if he died here, on this remote and rocky atoll, he'd never see Hilary's blue eyes again.

Coming back to Ottawa hadn't helped. In his store, in Domingo's, most of all in his apartment, he saw her, smelled her, imagined holding her in his arms. Imagined shaking her until she changed her mind and said she'd marry him.

Imagined uprooting her, dragging her with him across the globe. *Get real, MacDougall,* he told himself belligerently.

That's what it amounted to. It wasn't Mac she was turning down. It was the life he led, the career that had claimed him.

And now, in the midst of balloons and good beer and blazing red caftans and some of the most mouth-wateringly wonderful spicy hors d'oeuvres Mac had ever tasted, he suddenly asked himself whether, if Hilary didn't want his way of life, he even wanted it himself.

"A toast to Mac!" Domingo was shouting over the noise.

"Come on, Domingo. Toast somebody else for a change," Mac said, grinning tiredly.

"We didn't toast England yet." His friend grinned back. "To Mac's new job. To going to London. May he have enough adventures there to keep even himself satisfied!"

Loud cheers. Clinking of glasses, laughing and smiling and swaying to the rhythm of the steel band on the outdoor patio. Mac didn't hear any of it.

Adventures. What the hell had he been thinking of? He hadn't gone to work for External Affairs because he'd wanted a *job,* for God's sake. It had been the adventure that had lured him. And suddenly, in the space between one second and the next, Mac knew that his job wasn't an adventure anymore.

And furthermore, he knew where the adventure *was.*

"Thanks, everybody." He drained the last of the single beer he'd been nursing all evening, and set his glass down on the bar. "Gotta run, Domingo. Keep the party going, though, okay?"

There seemed to be no danger of it stopping. Judging from the rising noise level, there seemed virtually no chance that most of the guests would even notice he was gone. And that was just fine with him, because he had to get some things done in a hurry.

John Augustus Laurier MacDougall had just had another lightning flash.

* * *

"Hilary? I didn't know if I should bother you."

The voice was timid, and it belonged to one of her neighbors on the street, a single woman who kept an eagle eye on everything that went on in the vicinity.

"That's all right, Hazel. What's up?"

Hilary was sitting tiredly at her dining room table, experimenting with various arrangements of hot sauces in baskets. The photographer her graphic designer had lined up wanted to take pictures on Monday, and in the growing mountain of things to do, Hilary hadn't begun to contemplate exactly what she wanted pictures *of*. Hazel's call was an interruption she didn't really need.

"Well, it's just that there's a man sitting outside your store."

"A man? Well, it's a busy street, Hazel."

"But he's definitely sitting outside *your* store. I passed him on my way to the corner market, and he was still there when I passed by on my way home. And he has some tools with him."

That made her sit up straight. "What kind of tools?"

"Sharp things, you know, chisels and such. And I wasn't sure whether to just call the police, or you, or—"

"That's okay, Hazel. I'll check it out myself. Thanks for letting me know."

She hung up, cursing quietly under her breath. A break-in was all she needed right now. The store was full of new stock and new equipment, all purchased very much on spec. She couldn't afford to lose a penny's worth of it.

It seemed odd that a potential burglar would sit out on the sidewalk with his tools in plain view. But then, she hadn't had much experience with burglars. And it *was* getting late, almost ten-thirty, when Wellington Street started to be much less busy.

She wished Todd and Andrew were around, but the boys had gone to a school dance, and wouldn't be home for another hour. Hilary put on a coat over her sweater and jeans, and tossed a flashlight into her purse for good measure. With four heavy batteries aboard, the flashlight would make a passable weapon.

As soon as she approached the block where *Fortissimo* was, she could see that Hazel had been right. There *was* a man, sitting with his back to her. Definitely sitting, she noted, as though he had a camp stool with him or something. And he was strangely hunched over, digging or pushing at an object in his lap.

She could see a dark box on the sidewalk beside him. A toolbox, she thought, and frowned. This was even stranger than Hazel's call had led her to expect. Why should anyone park themselves and their toolbox on the sidewalk in front of her store, right under a streetlight, at ten-thirty on a Saturday night?

She'd stopped to put the question to herself, and now she hesitated before starting to walk again. In that instant's hesitation, the man half turned to look up at *Fortissimo*'s sign. And she caught a glimpse of his handsome face and the way his hair curled down onto his forehead.

Her heart jumped, and seemed to turn itself over. She put a hand up to her throat, as if she might be able to catch the startled cry that began to form there.

She wasn't quick enough. The sound escaped her, and he turned all the way around.

He was wearing a heavy gold canvas jacket, with a green plaid work shirt underneath. There was something large and flat sitting on his knees, and his boots were covered in wood shavings.

She didn't notice all those things at first. She noticed only his eyes, the openness of them, the lurking humor she loved, the serious purpose she'd learned was so unbendable. For a long moment she just stood and looked at him, not caring why he was here or whether he might vanish in a puff of smoke at any second. Mirage or not, she was heartachingly glad to see him, and there was no power in the world that could have made her admit otherwise.

Then he moved, and for the first time she noticed the big flat piece of wood in his lap. He set it down, and stood up, still holding her gaze.

Their eyes were sending each other a thousand signals a second. Are you all right? Are you glad to see me? Did you miss me? What are you doing here? The questions zipped back and forth over the empty space between them.

No answers were forthcoming. They were going to have to use words for that. Hilary heard Mac clear his throat, and noticed, wonderingly, that his hands seemed to be shaking. Her own had started to tremble with nerves and surprise and pain and the sweet anticipation of touching him again, the instant she'd recognized him.

"You got here too soon," he said, with a manful stab at his old glib style. "I was going to finish this up before I called you."

"You were spotted," she told him. "Not much of an undercover job you're doing here, is it?"

He looked ruefully at the tools and shavings around him. "I couldn't think how else to do it," he said. "I couldn't remember the design exactly, and when I looked around home, I realized I had nothing with your logo on it. So I had to come and copy it in person."

Hilary took three steps closer to him. She could see now that the flat piece of wood was roughly the same size as the carved sign that hung over *Fortissimo*'s door. She could also see rough pencil lines where Mac had sketched a copy of her design. Bold chisel strokes showed where he'd started to carve his copy.

"Mac, this is very strange, even for you," she told him. "Why are you copying my sign?"

"Well, it's not an exact copy." He held up the new piece of wood. "See, I had to leave room for the Roman numeral."

She peered at it. Peering involved getting a bit closer. She could feel the tug of his closeness now, the way she had every time since the first day she'd encountered him. She wanted to tell him to put down the sign, to forget about his explanation—which was obviously more complicated than she felt up to dealing with at the moment—and just hold her against him the way she'd been longing to have him do.

There was no way she could say any of that. She forced herself to sound at least halfway coherent. "It says *'Fortissimo II,'*" she read out loud. "I didn't realize I was planning an annex."

"Well, it's a good thing I'm around to tell you, isn't it?" He was grinning now, the cocky devil.

A thought assailed her suddenly, bringing with it a memory of the pain she'd felt in the ten days since she'd seen him last. "You're not still thinking about my moving to London, are you?" she demanded. "That just can't work, Mac. I meant what I said."

"I know you did." He set the sign down gently. "I should have listened when you said it the first time."

"Then what—"

"Shh." He cut off her question and stepped closer to her in the same moment. "I'll explain it, Hilary. I promise. But first, I'm going to go nuts if I don't kiss you in the next ten seconds."

She'd been thinking the same thing herself. And if she'd been in danger of losing her reason before, the danger tripled in the moment when he reached for her, pulled her against him, claimed her lips as though he had a right to all of her, as though he were coming home.

Hilary let herself sink deep into the kiss, savoring him, not caring what else was going on in Mac's mind or in the world around them. It was a pleasure tinged with pain, a wild jumble of feelings that gave a new edge to passion and a new meaning to desire.

They were both breathing hard by the time Mac lifted his lips far enough to say, "Well, that answers my first question, which is whether you would be happy to see me."

"'Happy' isn't the word I would have picked," she told him. She loosened her hold on him slightly; somehow her arms seemed to have fastened themselves around his neck as though she were clinging to a lifeline.

"No? How would you describe it?"

Hilary sighed. He was blunt, this pirate of hers, but never easy. "Relieved, that you didn't just disappear out of my life," she confessed. "Confused about what you think you're doing here. And mad as hell about the way you left."

He brushed a gentle hand over her cheekbone and Hilary hummed inside with the suggestiveness of it. "I shouldn't have roared off that way," he said softly. "But I felt like I'd offered you the world and you'd just turned it down flat. I was mad, too."

"Tell me about it. You blew such a cloud of smoke out of that old bike of yours, I think some of it's *still* hanging around the neighborhood."

That got a faint grin out of him. Only a faint one, though. Whatever he'd come here to say or do, it was something serious.

"Needs a tune-up," he commented. "Has for ten years now. I just never seem to be around long enough to get to it."

Hilary's heart caught in her throat again. What was he trying to tell her here? She didn't think she could stand the pain of another goodbye. But if leaving was what was on his mind, then what was the malarkey with the signs all about?

"All right, MacDougall, you got an answer to your first question," she said. "How about answering one of mine?"

"Fire away."

She pulled out of his arms and stood looking at the sign he'd propped against his folding stool. "What were you doing with that sign?" she asked.

He grinned outright now. "Carving," he said.

"No kidding. Care to tell me why?"

"Uh-uh. You got your answer. Now it's my turn. Did you get the hot sauce I asked my mother to bring over?"

"She came on Monday. Now do I get to ask another question?"

That grin of his was too enticing to be true. It drew her in, catching her in some undertow of longing that she didn't quite understand but would have been quite happy to spend the rest of her life trying to fathom.

"Why are you here, Mac?"

Her voice shook a bit as she asked it. She wasn't sure she really wanted to know. She *was* sure how good it felt to be with him again, but if he was only going to waltz out of her life again, she didn't think she could stand it.

He shoved his hands into the pocket of his old jacket, and took a couple of restless steps. "One, because I wanted to see you," he said.

She didn't answer. She waited, trying to guess what direction the wind was blowing from.

"Two, because I had news for you about my store."

"You're keeping it open?" She couldn't help the wild hope that sprang up in her.

"Well, no." Hope died a crashing death, and she clamped down on her feelings again, telling herself just to wait. "As you pointed out, I'm no businessman. But the place is set up to sell hot sauces now, and people know it's there. I hated the idea of closing it up and having some trendy little bistro take over. So I'm handing the lease over to *Fortissimo*."

"Mac, I can't afford that!"

He waved away her protest. "Pretty soon you'll be able to," he said. "It's a great location. You can't keep people away. And before long you'll be dragging in the big bucks from all those mail orders of yours. It's a golden opportunity, and I'm not going to let you pass it by." He frowned at her suddenly, and she felt the full force of his personality. "I thought you'd learned to take chances, if nothing else, in the past few months," he said.

"I thought so, too." Hilary spoke slowly, still not sure where he was headed. "But I have a feeling all I've really learned is how high the cost of taking a chance can be." She gave a laugh that threatened to choke her voice. "And I knew that already. Funny how I forgot all those lessons around you, isn't it?"

He wasn't grinning now. "I'm glad *you* find it funny," he said darkly. She was about to hit him with another question when he went on, "Anyway, the sign is for you. *Fortissimo the Second,* and long may it blister people's palates." He cleared his throat. "It's kind of a going-away present, I guess. I didn't want to leave things the way they were the last time we saw each other."

That was it, then. He was going away. He'd come here to make this gesture, because he was good-hearted and aboveboard and because she really had meant something to him. But he was still going away.

She felt a black wave of despair washing over her, and there was nothing she could do to hide it. When she'd seen him sitting on the sidewalk, she'd allowed herself to hope that he'd come back for good. And now he'd just said, matter-of-factly, that he hadn't.

"Oh, Mac..."

There was a desperate longing in her voice. She saw his head snap sharply up at her words, and watched his hazel eyes darken and his taut body shift position subtly, as if he'd just heard a warning bell clang in the distance.

Yet when he spoke, he seemed to choose his words carefully. "Of course," he said, "if you want to change your mind and marry me after all, I wouldn't have to hurry with the sign."

She felt her eyes widen in a hurry. They'd been on their way to filling with tears, but his words shocked the idea right out of her head. "The sign—what are you talking about?"

Why did he keep confusing things with the sign? She stepped closer to him, as if she might be able to read the answer in his eyes.

All she got was the ghost of a grin. "Well, if I stayed in Ottawa, and we ran these two stores together, then I wouldn't have to rush to get the sign done, and I could do a proper job on it."

"Would you stop talking about that damn sign?" Hope was fighting with despair now, and frustration was overriding both of them. "Mac, I thought it was all set that you were going to London."

"I thought it was, too. And External Affairs still thinks it's all set." The smile reached his lips now. "But let me tell you a very short, very sweet story, Hilary. I was standing in the middle of a party last night, a party in my honor, and there were all these people toasting the things I'd done and the things I was going to do, and all of a sudden I knew that if God or External Affairs or the man in the moon gave me a choice of anywhere in the world I'd rather be, the only place that sprung to mind was right here. Here in Ottawa, with you."

She hauled in a breath so deep her ribs ached with the effort. "This is moonshine, MacDougall," she said.

"Of the very highest and purest quality," he confirmed. "And it's also plain old common sense."

"Quitting your job? Abandoning your career? *That's* common sense?"

"Sure, when I've got another one all lined up that appeals to me far more than a life in the diplomatic corps does at the moment. Hilary, listen to me." He took his hands out of his pockets and waved them in the air as he spoke, sketching the future in the light of the street lamp. "I'm getting too old to be flying single-engine airplanes into cliffs on tropical islands. And I'm never going to settle down and be the kind of team-player diplomat my father was. So what's left?"

"A new adventure." Hilary breathed out the words, and saw him nod.

"And there's one just waiting for me," he said. "What could be more of an adventure than you and I scooping the hot sauce market just as it gets trendy? Or flying all over the place on buying trips? What could possibly be more of a challenge than being a father to two kids who can probably already beat me at arm wrestling?" He grinned wryly. "Antiaircraft fire pales when I compare it with that, believe me. And what could be more exciting than being married to you, I've been asking myself? And the answer is nothing. There's nothing in the world I want to do more than be with you, Hilary. There's nowhere in the world I want to be except where you are."

The tide was rising, carrying her with it. She felt him gather her in his arms again, felt the warm brush of his lips against her mouth. "Buying trips, you said?" She knew it sounded crazy, but they were the only words she could force out at the moment.

"Buying trips to the islands where they have oceans the color of your eyes and miles of sand the color of your skin." He ran a possessive hand over her hip, and she knew intimately, achingly, the colors he was thinking of. "Islands where the chili peppers aren't nearly as spicy as your smile."

She was smiling through a haze of tears at him now. "It's a good thing I already like hot food, isn't it?" she said.

"A darn good thing. Because if you hadn't, I might never have found you. And I would have missed the greatest adventure of my life."

His kiss was warm and persuasive. Hilary let herself be persuaded by it, let herself believe finally that what he was saying was true: he'd sailed into harbor happy—and more than happy—to come home at last. Home to her.

"You are the damnedest scoundrel, MacDougall," she told him, between kisses.

"Does that mean you'll marry me after all?"

"Yes." She grinned despite her tears. "And the people who make up clichés are wrong, Mac. It's not variety that's the spice of life." She traced a finger lovingly over his brow, over the laugh lines at the corners of his eyes, over the curve of his lips. "It's you, Mac. It's you."

They were standing on a street in Ottawa, flooded by the light from a street lamp above them. There was no earthly way, Hilary knew, that she could be tasting a salt breeze or feeling a ship's deck sway under her feet. It must be her own happy tears, and the sudden lightening of her heart when she looked into Mac's eyes and saw all her own hopes for their future reflected back at her.

There was no earthly way, but somehow she was sure she heard the sharp crack of a mainsail as it filled with a favorable wind and embarked on a new voyage with all its flags flying free.

* * * * *

Silhouette Special Edition

salutes

MOMENTS OF GLORY

from Lindsay McKenna

In a country torn with conflict, in a time of bitter passions, these brave men and women wage a war against all odds... and a timeless battle for honor, for fleeting moments of glory, for the promise of enduring love.

February: RIDE THE TIGER (#721) Survivor Dany Villard is wise to the love-'em-and-leave-'em ways of war, but wounded hero Gib Ramsey swears she's captured his heart... forever.

March: ONE MAN'S WAR (#727) The war raging inside brash and bold Captain Pete Mallory threatens to destroy him, until Tess Ramsey's tender love guides him toward peace.

April: OFF LIMITS (#733) Soft-spoken Marine Jim McKenzie saved Alexandra Vance's life in Vietnam; now he needs her love to save his honor....

SEMG-1

Silhouette Romance®

LONG, TALL TEXANS

DONAVAN
Diana Palmer

Diana Palmer's bestselling LONG, TALL TEXANS series continues with DONAVAN....

From the moment elegant Fay York walked into the bar on the wrong side of town, rugged Texan Donavan Langley knew she was trouble. But the lovely young innocent awoke a tenderness in him that he'd never known...and a desire to make her a proposal she couldn't refuse....

Don't miss DONAVAN by Diana Palmer, the ninth book in her LONG, TALL TEXANS series. Coming in January...only from Silhouette Romance.

LTT192

Coming in February from

SILHOUETTE® Desire™

MAN OF THE MONTH

THE BLACK SHEEP
by Laura Leone

Man of the Month Roe Hunter
wanted nothing to do with
free-spirited Gingie Potter.

Yet beneath her funky fashions
was a woman's heart—and body—
he couldn't ignore.

You met Gingie in
Silhouette Desire #507
A WILDER NAME
also by Laura Leone
Now she's back.

SDBL

YOU'VE ASKED FOR IT,
YOU'VE GOT IT! MAN OF THE MONTH: 1992

ONLY FROM
SILHOUETTE® *Desire*™

You just couldn't get enough of them, those sexy men from Silhouette Desire—twelve sinfully sexy, delightfully devilish heroes. Some will make you sweat, some will make you sigh . . . but every long, lean one of them will have you swooning. So here they are, men we couldn't resist bringing to you for one more year. . . .

A KNIGHT IN TARNISHED ARMOR
by Ann Major in January

THE BLACK SHEEP
by Laura Leone in February

THE CASE OF THE MESMERIZING BOSS
by Diana Palmer in March

DREAM MENDER
by Sheryl Woods in April

WHERE THERE IS LOVE
by Annette Broadrick in May

BEST MAN FOR THE JOB
by Dixie Browning in June

Don't let these men get away! *Man of the Month*, only in Silhouette Desire.